CW00411508

HIDDEN ELEMENTS

By Bradley James Moore

ARTWORK BY DEAN HANNON

Chapter One:

The First Victim

"Five ft five inches, Female, twenty-eight, Blonde, Caucasian"

"thank you" said Steven discerningly as he knelt towards the young woman's corpse. Steven analysed the body for a few moments, then returned to an upright position.

"Do we know the cause of death?" he asked the forensic scientist who had previously given him information about the body.

"She was strangled then stabbed with a metal pipe through the back, which punctured her left lung, causing it to fill with blood" he responded whilst pointing to the pipe, which had been carefully bagged for evidence.

"And when was the body found?" Steven asked as he walked towards the bagged murder weapon and held it aloft to examine it. The bright, strong, early sunlight beamed between the high-rise buildings either side of the alleyway that formed the crime scene, helping to illuminate the evidence and allow Steven to gain a better view.

"three o'clock this morning"

"and when was she killed?"

"I'd place time of death around one-two hours before the body was found" responded the on-site scientist.

"Why is the pipe an odd colour?" Steven asked as he noticed the colour of the pipe was different to the ones, he had seen at his local home store.

"the odd thing is it's made from germanium" he said with a hint of confidence.

Steven stared for a while "what's germanium?" he expressed with a hint of scornfulness.

The scientist removed his glasses breathed on the glass centres and used his jacket to polish the lenses. "it's a greyish-white metalloid like silicon or tin. It is used more commonly as a semiconductor in transistors and various other electronical devices."

Stevens expression remained the same "well… no-one saw anything and there were no cameras fixed on this alleyway" said a tall, thin blonde man walking towards Steven, as he ducked beneath the police tape to enter the crime scene, "but we do have a home address and a place of work."

"Good work Geoffrey" said Steven "I'm not surprised we have no witnesses, have you noticed how quiet the roads are either side of this alleyway?", Steven responded as he moved his head from either side of the crime scene. The distinct lack of noise from cars racing by or the chatter of the public made it easy for them to hear one another.

"yeah" Geoffrey answered, "the killer must have planned it… or just got lucky."

"Shall we check out her home address?" Steven asked as he turned and walked to the squad car at the end of the alleyway. Geoffrey followed as he gave a nod of departure to the forensic scientist, who nodded in return.

The two detectives entered the vehicle and began to drive towards the next point of interest. "what are your initial thoughts?" Steven asked Geoffrey, as he took the next left at the set of traffic lights. Steven was the primary detective on the case whilst Geoffrey was the secondary. Steven liked to encourage Geoffrey to give his thoughts and opinions on cases to help develop his skillset.

"The killer was drunk and was provoked to murder; this is evident by the messy nature of the murder, and the time it occurred. Perhaps a night on the town gone sour." The killer got lucky with the location, however, can't imagine their being much foot traffic at that time of night."

"Very lucky" responded Steven "no witnesses, no cameras and no traces left at the crime scene, hopefully they pull some prints off the murder weapon. They were either intoxicated and lucky or this was pre-meditated."

"Perhaps your right"

Steven looked at Geoffrey and smirked "I'm usually right." Steven had been a detective for fifteen years, ten more than Geoffrey, and had a wealth of experience he was trying to pass onto him, when Geoffrey could be bothered to listen.

"It is just up here, on the left" Geoffrey said as he pointed to a tall block of apartments. Steven pulled the car up to the front of the building, exited the vehicle and walked towards the apartment block. Steven held the door open and gestured Geoffrey into the building "why thank you sir" Geoffrey sarcastically quipped as he crossed the threshold of the building. Steven and Geoffrey climbed the square spiral staircase to the third floor "room forty-two" said Geoffrey as he referenced his notebook. Steven knocked on the door and turned towards Geoffrey "let me do the talking", Geoffrey raised his right eyebrow as the door slowly opened. "Hello, does a Miss Willow live here?" the man nodded his head in bemusement, Steven reached to his waist and pulled his ID from his hip and held it high. "I'm detective Steven Cooper and this is my partner Geoffrey Osbourne, may we come in?"

"o.. of.. of course," the man stammered as he opened his door wider. The two detectives took a seat beside one another on the tan leather sofa as the man sat in an upright armchair. "are you Miss Willow's partner?" questioned Steven

"no, she's my roommate and please call me Paul, Paul Freeman" Mr Freeman responded.

"And what is your relation to her Paul?"

"We're friends, we met at university and around two years ago we decided to rent an apartment together, may I ask what all this is about?" Paul asked with concern.

"I'm sorry to have to tell you this but Miss Willow was found dead around three A.M. this morning, I'm sorry for your loss" Steven responded sympathetically as Paul slumped in his chair.

"There must be a mistake! I saw her last night, before she left to meet her friends at a bar."

"And the fact she hadn't returned that night didn't worry you?"

"she often stayed out late and would stay at a friend's house… or with a guy she had met." Paul responded as he rose from his armchair to get a glass of water from the open plan kitchen. "can I get either one of you anything?" Paul asked

"no, we're fine" replied Geoffrey as he rose from his seat and began inspecting the apartment. "You don't mind if I look around, do you?" Queried Geoffrey

"Go Ahead" Paul replied.

Geoffrey headed to one of the adjoining rooms which happened to be the bedroom of Miss Willow. He was greeted by a stale smell which suggested a window had not been opened in a while. The blue carpet was barely visible through the discarded clothes that lay on the floor, the blinds were closed making it harder for Geoffrey to make out finer details. He flicked the light switch and immediately noticed the row of empty spirit bottles that lined her windowsill. He walked towards them and picked one up, it peeled away from the surface suggesting the bottle had been there a while. He placed it back down and headed to her bed side table where he saw three passport photos, one had been cut out and removed. He looked up and realised there were no family photos dotted around or hung up, the walls were empty. Geoffrey took the photos back into the living where Mr Freeman was trying to calm himself down.

"Did Miss Willow have any family members?" Geoffrey asked.

"Yeah, but her and her parents did not see eye to eye, they weren't fond of her party lifestyle and excessive drinking. I can't remember the last time she spoke to them, must have been around Christmas, the one time of year they see each other."

"I think we've pestered Mr Freeman enough, come on Geoffrey" Steven expressed as he rose from his seat.

"Can I take one of these photos?" Geoffrey asked holding the passport photos he had collected earlier.

"Ummm sure" Paul responded quietly.

The two men left the apartment, headed downstairs and back into car. "What did you find in the bedroom?" Steven asked

"it was messy, very messy. No personal effects, family photos or memento's, lots of empty spirit bottles, which had been there a while, something told me she didn't spend much time in her bedroom."

"Hopefully, her work can tell us more" Said Steven as he checked his watch, which Geoffrey noticed.

They arrived at a solicitor's office three roads away, they exited the car and entered the lobby of the offices. Greeted by a cheerful smart dressed brunette on reception "hi, how can I help you" she replied. Before Steven could respond Geoffrey smirked and said, "does a Miss Willow work here?" as he leaned in closer to the receptionist.

"Yes, however she is not in today, I can refer you to another solicitor if you'd like?" she responded gesturing to the phone.

"That would be helpful" Steven retorted glaring at Geoffrey as he did. Steven Did not like Geoffrey flirting with people whilst working, he knew Geoffrey was passionate about his job. But sometimes he acted like it was a game.

The receptionist picked up the phone and before she had placed it down a short, well dressed bald man arrived in the foyer to greet them. "hey, how can I be of assistance?" said the gentleman with a cheery nature. Steven displayed his badge and said,

"I'm detective Steven Cooper and this is my partner detective Geoffrey Osbourne, were here to talk about miss Willow."

"what has she done now?" asked the solicitor as he gestured them into a meeting room, Geoffrey stopped before entering "mind if I look around?" he asked whilst gesticulating his hand in a circular motion. "of course," replied the solicitor as he and Steven entered the meeting room and closed the door behind them.

Geoffrey walked down the well-lit corridor and followed the building round to the left where he saw a closed door with the name 'miss Penelope Willow' centred. He opened the door and began to look around the office, he noticed a faint smell of alcohol in the air. He walked round behind the desk and saw a photo of Miss Willow and Mr Freeman at their graduation. It was the only photo on her desk or on the walls for that matter, other than her framed law degree. Geoffrey began opening her drawers most of them were filled with scruffy paperwork except for the bottom. The bottom drawer contained a half empty gin bottle, Geoffrey looked around the room and noticed no glasses or mixer. Under the bottle of gin was a photo of the victim in what looked like her teenage years posing with her parents at what appeared to be a new year's party. Geoffrey closed the door and walked to the closed blinds, he separated them with his right index finger and peered through the opening he had created. He looked out onto a wonderful view of a well blossomed courtyard in the centre of the office blocks, filled with benches and busy bird feeders. He saw the dust build-up on the windowsill, the blinds were not opened often if at all. "Got all you need" Steven asked as he appeared at the entrance to the office and checked his watch again, "yeah" responded Geoffrey, they began to exit the building. As they left Geoffrey winked at the receptionist at the front desk, which annoyed Steven.

As the pair entered the vehicle Steven glared at Geoffrey. "You know I don't like it when you do that" Steven said with a serious tone

"do what?" Geoffrey asked rhetorically.

"You know what" Steven said as he raised an eyebrow in Geoffrey's direction while Geoffrey shrugged.

"What did solicitor have to say" asked Geoffrey trying to distract Steven from the topic at hand.

"Apparently her not showing up for work was becoming a regular occurrence. However, he seemed genuinely shocked when I told him about Miss Willow. What did you find in the office?"

"very little personal effects and another spirit bottle, This one a little more hidden."

"Just like her bedroom, sounds like she is an alcoholic, all the signs are a little too familiar. She probably found a way to function, but perhaps things were getting too much."

"Also, her blinds were closed and looked like they hadn't been opened in a while. Her office looked onto a lovely, relaxing courtyard why wouldn't someone what to see that?"

"The light probably didn't sit well with her when she came into work drunk and continued her drinking." Steven said as he checked his watch for the third time.

"Oh, right you've got his awards ceremony tonight, that's why you keep checking you watch. Have you prepared you speech, don't forget to thank me" chuckled Geoffrey.

"The speech is ready; I just don't like public speaking it makes me nervous."

"You'll do fine just run on stage, thank everyone, and run off again, simple as that"

"thanks for the advice, just drop me home" Steven sighed.

Chapter Two:
Awards Night

Geoffrey pulled up outside Stevens family home, a modest two-bedroom house with a narrow driveway and a small front garden. Steven exited the vehicle and walked up the concrete pathway towards his home. "See you tonight!" yelled Geoffrey as he wheeled up the passenger side window Steven had left open, before speeding off.

As Steven entered his home, he was greeted by his young daughter running up to him and hugging him round his waist. His wife appeared at the top of the stairs looking down at him whilst fixing her earing. "It's six o'clock we need to be there for seven" called down Stevens wife, Steven looked up. He could not help but notice how beautiful she looked, long flowing blonde hair draped over her tanned shoulders, bright blue eyes above an immaculate smile.

She was wearing a slim red cocktail dress and tall high heels. "Are you listening to me" she called again still fixing her earring. Steven shook his head out of his trance, released his daughter's python-like grip on him. "Daddy's got to get ready, go play in the living room" he said as he gestured to the room on his left and ran up the stairs. He kissed his wife on the cheek as he passed and headed for the shower.

"how do I look Claire?" asked Steven as he joined his wife and daughter in the living room dressed for the evenings event. Claire looked him up and down, his usually scruffy short brown hair was styled neatly, his stubbled face now clean shaven and his blue eyes stood out due to the black tuxedo he was wearing. Suddenly the doorbell went, and Claire clambered to the front door. "Hiya" Claire said excitedly to the babysitter who was there to look after their daughter. "Lily" she yelled "Sarah's here, be a good girl", both Claire and Steven left the house and travelled to the city hall where the awards ceremony was being held. "try to look happy darling" Claire expressed to Steven "after all, you are receiving an award tonight."

Steven sighed "I know that's the problem I'm not great at public speaking."

"you'll do fine" said Claire as she kissed him on the cheek. "Let's just try to enjoy the evening."

The couple entered the large city hall which was packed with around two-hundred and fifty people, enough chairs to seat every one of them and around twenty to twenty-five large round tables. The couple promptly found their seats and began to converse with their dinner guests. The food was served quickly, a three-course meal of tomato soup, ox cheek, spinach and ricotta cannelloni for Claire as she was vegetarian and white chocolate and raspberry crème brulee for dessert. Once the tables were cleared, a tall round man took to the stage located at the head of the room.

"Hello and welcome to the annual Hightower police department awards ceremony" he bellowed across the room assisted by the onstage microphone. "This is where we honour

our hardworking and devoted employees of the H.T.P.D", Steven turned his chair to gain a better view of the stage. "Any wine sir" a waiter asked Steven as he gestured towards his empty glass. "No thanks, I'm fine with water" Steven replied as he raised his water glass to his lips.

"Also don't forget to by some raffle tickets as they circulate, all the proceeds go to local charities" the on-stage host said with a huge grin. "Now without further ado let's give away some of these awards", several moments passed and the table, which was full of plaques at the beginning of the night was starting to thin.

"The award for employee of the year as voted for by the rest of the team, goes to a man who I know has overcome personal difficulties and worked incredibly hard during his time at the force". The tall round man leant over to pick up a plaque and repositioned his mouth in front of the microphone again. "He has been supported heavily by his family and his quirky partner, I'm sure he won't mind me saying that." A low groan of laughter waved across the audience, "detective Steven Cooper, please give him a round of applause." A loud procession of claps accompanied Steven as he made his way through the tables towards the stage. He slowly took the award from the evening host and paused for a photo. He positioned himself in front of the microphone and let out a slow sigh as he adjusted the height of the stand.

"I would firstly like to thank everyone who voted for me, to be voted employee of the year by your colleagues is truly a special honour. I would like to thank my partner Geoffrey who has been by my side for the past three years. We started out a little rocky and although he infuriates me most of the time, I wouldn't change him for anyone." The crowd chuckled as Geoffrey raised his pint glass towards Steven and nodded his head. "And last but certainly not least, my beautiful wife Claire. What can I say about Claire, she makes me want to be a better man, I honestly do not know where I would be if it wasn't for her? Not standing here that is for sure, I love you Claire." Steven emoted as a tear slowly trickled down his face.

"Thank you all" Steven exited the stage to another round of applause.

As he was walking back to his table, he saw a young man talking to his wife, he thought he recognised him but could not put his finger on it. Just before he had a good view of the man, he felt a hand grasp his shoulder, he turned to see an officer he knew from his precinct reaching out to shake his hand. "Congratulations Steven" he said cheerfully "let me buy you a drink"

"thank you, but I don't drink" Steven responded.

"Oh, since when? if you don't mind me asking"

"I've been sober for five years now" Steven said humbly,

"Well good for you Steven" the man said before patting Steven on the shoulder and walking back to his table. Steven copied him, as he turned back the mysterious man had left the table.

"who was that?" Steven asked as he took his seat and placed his award on the table.

"He was selling raffle tickets, I bought Five" Claire responded as she raised the tickets so Steven could see them better.

"It's funny I thought I recognised him, but I must be mistaken" Steven said as he shook his head.

"Now time for the raffle" called the ceremony host, twenty-five minutes past of prizes being won and distributed. "Now for the main prize, two tickets to the new botanical gardens known as 'Genesis'. Be among the first people into the gardens, the tickets include a tour of the grounds, advice from some of the leading botanical experts on growing your own flowers and a moonlit dinner. Truly an amazing prize" the room fell silent as the host pulled the ticket up to his face. "And the winner is pink no.345, I'll read that again pink no.345." Claire clutched at her tickets and yelled "we've won" as she shook Steven "go on, go get the prize" she said handing him the ticket and pushing him towards the stage. Steven Got up reluctantly and with a blushed face walked the same path back to the stage. Encouraged by his third applause of the evening he took the tickets from the host, turned to the audience and gave a cheesy grin before scurrying off the stage. "That concludes the nights entertainment, thank you to everyone who bought tickets and donated to these fabulous causes and please, drive home safe."

Geoffrey caught up to Steven and Claire before they left, "an award and the top prize you two really cleaned up tonight". Geoffrey said with a hint of intoxication

"you know you played a major part in me winning this award" Steven responded as grabbed Geoffrey by the shoulder. "I would not still be here if you didn't take that bullet for me all those years ago"

"Yeah, your right, and I'll never let you forget it" Geoffrey Smirked. Steven slowly let go, broke his eye contact, placed his arm around his wife's shoulder before saying "enjoy your weekend Geoffrey."

The Coopers arrived back home, relieved the babysitter of her duties and headed upstairs to check on their daughter. She was fast asleep "she's such an angel" whispered Claire to Steven as she slowly closed the bedroom door.

Chapter Three:

The Importance of Family

The next morning Steven was woken by a combination of sunlight peering through a gap in his blinds, hitting his eyes and the smell of breakfast being cooked by his wife. Steven leisurely swivelled sideways and sat up in his bed, he reached upwards and stretched out his arms and swayed laterally. He stood up and left his bedroom not before tripping on the shoes he had kicked off the night before. As he walked down the stairs, the sound of bacon sizzling was muffled by the music coming from the television. His daughter was watching her favourite Saturday morning cartoon. Steven slipped past without his daughter realising; he found his wife in a bath robe cooking bacon on the stove. He sauntered up behind her and hugged her, which startled her. His grip was tight, as he placed his head on her shoulder, she rested hers on his. "love you" he breathed in her ear and she echoed the words back. Suddenly Steven felt something grab hold of his side, he turned to see his daughter grasping his left leg, her long, light brown hair flowed either side of her big blue eyes. He knelt, picked her up and placed her on the kitchen unit. "What do you want to do today" Steven asked lovingly

"go to the park!" Lily responded with excitement

"then the park it is" replied Steven as he reached for the ketchup in the cupboard.

The family finished their bacon sandwiches, minus the crusts on Lily's plate, and prepared themselves for the day ahead.

They arrived at the local park around midday, Lily quickly ran towards the swing set as her mother shouted "slowdown", but Lily was out of earshot at this point. Steven smirked as he spotted an empty bench, they walked over and sat before it could be seized by other park goers. The bench was a perfect location to watch Lily playing in the park.

The park was filled with children playing joyfully, parents reluctantly joining in and babies screaming. The sound of children's laughter was drowned out by the repetitive barking of dogs crossing one another on the path in front of the bench. A large, open, green field occupied most of the park, large, tall oak trees framed the perimeter.

"Looking forward to getting back to work?" Steven asked Claire. Claire worked as a secondary school history teacher at Hightower community school, as it was the summer holiday's she was enjoying her time off.

"Yeah, I am" she replied, "I like being busy and I love teaching."

"And it will be even better next year when Lily starts"

"it will be" responded Claire. "Although I won't be teaching her, but I'll see her around the school."

"Dad come push me on the swings" yelled Lily towards Steven. Steven took his arm from his wife's shoulder, which he had placed there when the pair sat down and walked into the playground where the children were playing.

Claire watched on intently as the man she loved pushed her daughter on the swings, before giving it a go himself. A few moments past before Steven arrived back huffing and puffing "your turn" he said as he dropped to the bench. Claire obliged and made her way to the park.

Half an hour had passed, and Lily's energy was running out. Steven almost drifted off on the park bench, when he shot up to attention, he noticed a suspicion man across the field leaning against a tree. He stood up to gain a better view "Steven" yelled Claire, but Steven was mesmerised by the man. "Steven" Claire said as she reached his side with Lily, he turned towards her

"sorry dear, but does that look like the man from last night? The one who sold you the raffle tickets?"

"What man" Claire asked with perplexity, Steven turned back to find the man wasn't present anymore "no one" he said, as he walked towards the exit, periodically checking over his shoulder to see if the man had returned.

The family of three arrived back home, as they exited their family vehicle Stevens phone began to ring. He took it from his pocket and checked to see who it was, "it's Geoffrey" he said to his wife "go ahead I'll see what he wants." Claire and Lily walked toward the front door as Steven stayed by the car and answered the phone "Hey Geoffrey what's up?"

"We've got another lead on the willow case, Mr Freeman has put us onto a man she used to hook up with regularly" Geoffrey replied. Although it was the weekend, Geoffrey, being single, liked to put in extra hours at work, unless he was seeing another girl.

"That's great news" responded Steven "now stop working and relax, read a book, ride a bike do something other than work, let the weekend squad work the case. Go see that girl you told me about what was her name… Lucy?"

"Olivia, maybe another day, you're always going on about work life balance, I might just read a book", retorted Geoffrey sarcastically as he hung up the phone, Steven placed his phone in his pocket, waved to the neighbours and entered his house.

The next day went by quickly as Steven spent the day completing tasks at home, filing reports, which Claire hated him doing on his days off, and playing with his daughter in the garden.

As the Coopers sat down for dinner Steven walked into the living room and stopped by the CD player. He picked up a case from the cupboard below, removed the CD and slid it into the disk tray. He pressed play as he walked away, and Claire began to hear to sound of the music playing from the speaker. "I love Van Morrison" she said smiling at her husband, she began to sway as she placed out the food on the table. Lily quickly ate her food leaving the vegetables, "can I go play with my toys?" she asked.

"Finish your vegetables first" Claire said with authority

Lily huffed "fine", she scoffed down her broccoli and carrots before running off to her room. Steven and Claire slowly finished their food and conversed while the CD, that Steven put on, finished its last song. Claire looked at her watch "better go tell her to get ready for bed", Claire left the table, as she did Steven cleared the plates and put on the kettle. He made two boiling hot cups of tea and placed them on the glass coffee table in the living room. Claire came downstairs in her pink pyjamas just as Steven had started playing 'Children of the corn' on the television. Steven was a big fan of classic movies and loved to re-watch some of his favourites on Sunday evenings. "ooh I love this one" Claire said as she slumped onto the sofa and cuddled up to Steven.

The next morning Steven was woken by his six A.M. alarm, he rose from his slumber trying not to wake his still sleeping wife, jumped in the shower, headed downstairs to fill his takeaway coffee flask and left his home. As usual he waited outside for Geoffrey to pick him up, he saw the squad car coming down the street and eventually pulling up outside his house. He opened the door and fell into the passenger seat "made good time today, my coffee is still warm" Steven said with a smirk. Geoffrey lowered his sunglasses from the top of his head on to his eyes, smiled and pulled away from the curb.

"How was your weekend?" asked Geoffrey

"it was good thanks, went to the park, did some jobs around the house and spent time with family, what about yours?"

"pretty much the opposite of that" Geoffrey responded; the pair smiled at one another.

The two detectives arrived at the precinct to quickly check over some files on the case they were investigating, before leaving to investigate their new lead.

They arrived at a block of apartments one road away from the crime scene. "Convenient" Geoffrey said as he hit the buzzer allowing them to enter the building, they walked to the door of their lead and banged it hard three times "okay, okay sheesh!" responded a voice from behind the door. The sound of multiple locks loosening followed, and the door became slightly ajar. "what do you want" murmured the blonde wavy-haired man as he peered through the slight crack in the door. "I'm detect.." before Steven could finish his sentence the man slammed the door, the detectives stepped back. Geoffrey Took the sunglasses from his head and placed them on the neck of his shirt, with one swift motion he kicked the door right by the handle and created an opening for the detectives to enter through. Steven did not like how happy that made Geoffrey but couldn't deny he wished he could do it. The wavy-haired man became startled, held his hands up and said, "I wasn't the guy dealing drugs at Alexandra Place last night I swear!". The two detectives looked at each other, "that's not why we're here" Geoffrey expressed as he gestured towards to sofa, which was covered in dirty clothing. The man took a seat as the detectives remained standing, "I'm going to take a look around"

"and I'll finish what I started" said Steven poignantly "I'm detective Steven Cooper and this is detective Geoffrey Osbourne."

The man began breathing slower "am I supposed to be impressed?" he said disrespectfully.

"Do you know this girl" Steven raised a picture of Miss Willow, that he collected from the precinct earlier.

"Yeah I recognise her, but I haven't seen her in weeks" the man replied with a look of distain.

"Well she was found dead in an alleyway one road from here, we also have reason to believe you two met up often!" Expressed Steven with a stern tone of voice.

"What" yelled the wavy-haired man "I did not know she was dead, and I had nothing to do with it! We met in a club once, a few months back and we've been on and off ever since, but I didn't kill her if that's what you're saying!"

"Where were you around midnight on Friday?"

"I was D'Jing at 'The One Club' on Wilson Boulevard. I'm sure if you contact them, they will vouch for me, I also definitively didn't see her that night."

"So, when was the last time you saw Miss Willow?"

"I don't know, must have been a week or so ago, I don't keep a record."

The man's short snappy nature and impolite manner was starting to annoy Steven. Luckily enough he had got all the information he needed from him. Geoffrey re-entered the living room "nothing" he said walking towards Steven and assuming a position next to him. "You're not planning on leaving town anytime, soon are you?" Geoffrey questioned.

"No" replied the man nervously

"good" replied Geoffrey as he leaned in closer to the suspect. As the detectives left the building Geoffrey could not help himself by saying "sorry about the door" as he chuckled, Steven rolled his eyes.

The pair arrived back at the squad car and began their journey back to the precinct. "What do you make of him?" Geoffrey asked

"very disrespectful and highly annoying, but I don't think he's our man. I need you to check out his alibi when we get back to the precinct."

"Of course," replied Geoffrey.

Chapter Four:

The Second Victim

The two detectives arrived back at the precinct around one P.M, not before they had grabbed coffee on the way. As they walked into the bullpen of the precinct the door to the captain's office was wide open, and the head of the precinct was staring directly at them. "Why do I get the feeling he's annoyed at me" asked Geoffrey as the two men stood frozen in the middle of the room. With a slow movement the captain raised his arm and gestured for Geoffrey to join him in his office. "wish me luck" Geoffrey said as he gulped and shuffled towards the office door, Steven preceded to his desk and slumped in his chair.

Steven looked over Miss Willow's case file trying to see if he had missed anything. It's not usual for an opportunistic murder to turn up so little evidence, unless it was planned, he thought to himself. Geoffrey re-appeared from the captain's office with a sullen look, "what was that about?" asked Steven.

"Raymond's not happy with my paperwork, says a grown man should be able to file reports"

"well he's not wrong and you know he doesn't like you calling him by his first name", Steven quipped, Geoffrey shrugged his shoulders "I need you to check out that alibi" said Steven

"on it" Geoffrey responded as he made his way to his desk. Steven watched him take his seat, he could not help but notice how untidy Geoffrey's desk was. Unorganised paperwork, half eaten food and clothes sprawled over the surface. It was a stark contrast to Stevens desk which was meticulous, everything had a place, and everything was in its place.

Steven's thought process was interrupted by the on-duty sergeant in charge of the detective squad. "Got another case for you Steven, owner of M&T lighting supplies reported a body at his store this morning", Said the tall well-built sergeant "the scene has been cordoned off and forensics are already on the scene"

"Thanks sergeant" Steven responded as he packed away the files he was perusing. Steven rose from his desk and walked towards Geoffrey, "did the alibi check out?" asked Steven.

"Yeah multiple witnesses place him at 'The One Club' around the time of the murder" Geoffrey answered. "Also received news from the lab, they weren't able to pull prints from the weapon found in Miss Willow's body."

"Great news" Steven said sarcastically "get your coat we've got another case."

The pair left the precinct and headed towards to the new crime scene. This murder was suspiciously close to where the murder of Miss Willow took place. Hopefully, we can find more at the scene Steven thought to himself.

The pair pulled up to the crime scene, which was located at the end of a busy high-street, the scene had been cordoned off and the lab techs were sweeping the scene. A small crowd had gathered at the edge of the police tape and were being asked to get back. The high street was still busy with people as it was a popular shopping and dining location for the citizens of Hightower. As the detectives approached the scene Steven initially noticed the door to the store had been damaged around the lock but the rest of the building was still in intact. He saw the owner of the store standing to the side of the scene talking to a uniformed officer. "I'll speak to the owner whilst you investigate the scene" Steven said as the two split up to complete their respective tasks. "Hi, I'm detective Cooper, are you the store owner?" Steven asked the shaken man who was being warmed by a blanket draped over his shoulders.

"Yes, my name is David" he responded whilst trying to compose his self.

"Can I ask you a few questions?"

"sure" responded David whilst removing the blanket that was draped over his shoulders.

"when and how did you find the body?"

"around nine-thirty this morning, I arrived to open the store, noticed the lock had been broken and saw the body on the floor", David replied taking a deep breath.

"Do you recognise the victim?"

"yeah, he's a homeless man who liked to sleep in the alcove of my store at night."

"And does that bother you?" asked Steven pryingly

"not particularly, he didn't cause disturbances often and he would make himself scarce during opening hours."

"Didn't cause disturbances often?" Steven encouraged

"when he had a good day begging, for lack of a better word, he would buy himself alcohol from the shop across the way. I must admit I gave him my loose change often. Once or twice he entered the store shouting and slurring his words. I always managed to get him to leave without having to call the police though."

"do you know his name?"

"no, we just had an unspoken mutual understanding."

"Do you have any security footage which might help the case?"

"there is a camera focused on the front of the store, but I don't have internal cameras, sorry" the man responded apologetically.

"Thanks for your help" Steven said before heading to join Geoffrey on the scene.

Steven entered the store, "god, those lights are bright" he exclaimed as he shielded his eyes. The back wall of the building was covered in bright multicoloured lights beaming towards the entrance.

"Neon" Geoffrey responded, "takes me back to my clubbing days."

Steven smirked "what have we got?"

"adult male, between thirty and forty years of age, six foot two, no wallet or personal effects. A DNA swab has been taken to try and get a positive ID."

"Makes sense" Steven responded "the owner mentioned he was homeless so can't imagine he had too many personal items. How was he killed?"

"asphyxiation, but no prints left on the neck" Geoffrey replied, "but here's the odd thing, he was murdered somewhere else, my guess is nearby and transported here."

"That is odd, why murder someone in one place and move them to another to be found". Steven asked rhetorically

"exactly" Geoffrey exclaimed "than explains why there is no sign of a struggle, the door is busted but no other damage. Also, some of the electricals in here are worth hundreds maybe even thousands but none have been reported stolen."

"That is strange" agreed Steven "the store clerk mentioned a camera positioned outside the store hopefully that will give us more to go on" informed Steven.

Steven acquired the tapes and headed back to the precinct with Geoffrey. Was this victim selected or just random, why was he moved to that store, and why was nothing stolen Steven thought to himself. So many unanswered questions, hopefully the video tapes answered them.

They arrived back at the precinct, took up position at Stevens desk and uploaded the footage they obtained from the store front. A few moments past before Steven found the footage from nine thirty that morning, around the time the clerk discovered the body, he began to rewind to see what they could find.

"Stop, go back" Geoffrey shouted. Steven stopped the tape, and slowly re-wound it. They both leaned in closer to get a better view. The camera's footage was hazy at best and the quality was affected by the bright neon lights emanating from the store.

"Those bloody neon lights" Steven said, "they're making it hard to see." Geoffrey had spotted something, two men walking towards the front of the store, one was clearly the victim the other was harder to make out. His face was hidden by a balaclava and a long-hooded coat masked the rest of his body. The mysterious man looked like he was helping an intoxicated John Doe walk down the high street before stopping in front of the shop window. The bright lights coming from the structure prevented the detectives from seeing anymore. "To me it looks like this is our murderer" said Geoffrey "he must have strangled our victim elsewhere and walked him down the street like he was drunk, as to not arouse suspicion, broke into the store and discarded the body".

"But why this store?" asked Steven "and did he know the lights would have obscured the camera footage?"

"He must have known otherwise why move the body at all" Geoffrey responded.

The tapes seemed to generate more questions for Steven and Geoffrey to answer. "I think we need to find where he killed the victim, that will help us answer some of these questions" Steven assessed.

Five o'clock struck and the two detectives finished up and began their journey home, Geoffrey dropped Steven off outside his house like he did every day. Geoffrey sped off in the squad car.

As Steven walked to his front door, he noticed an envelope stuck to his door handle. He picked it up, looked at it quizzically and began to open it slowly whilst checking over his shoulders skittishly. In the envelope was piece of paper with only three words typed in the middle 'Recognise me yet?'. Steven stared at the paper as if he were in a trance, when suddenly the front door opened and startled him. "Honey what are you doing standing on the doorstep?" his wife asked whilst raising an eyebrow inquisitively. "Nothing" he replied, stuffing the paper into his coat pocket, brushing past her and kissing her on the cheek. He took his coat off and placed it on the rack adjacent to the stairs, "what's for dinner?" he asked excitedly.

Chapter Five:
Old Friends

The Coopers sat that evening for dinner, Claire had prepared a vegetable curry complete with samosa's and naan bread. "What did you do with mum today?" Steven asked Lily as he dipped his naan in some mango chutney.

"We went to the history museum and looked at old things" she responded sourly.

"you said you enjoyed it" Claire responded, "you liked the Egyptian section with all the mummies."

"it was ok I guess" said Lily as she pushed the chickpeas and lentils round her plate.

"Face it Claire, she's not as interested in history as you are, maybe one day" Steven said to console his wife. "You know Lily, if you enjoy history and select it as one of your studies, in a few years' time you'll have mum as your teacher."

"But history is boring" replied Lily as she finished the food on her plate.

"Hey, I tried" Steven shrugged as Claire smiled at him.

The family finished their meals, Claire cleaned the plates and they sat down to watch some television before bed.

Steven awoke the next day at six o'clock like every morning, he had had a terrible night sleep. He could not stop thinking about the letter he found on his front door the evening before. He laid in bed for a few moments staring at the ceiling, who could the note be from? was it the man from the awards ceremony and the park? was It the man from the video footage? Were they the same person? all these thoughts swirled around his mind. He rose from his king-sized bed and readied himself for work, kissed his wife on the forehead whilst she slept and headed downstairs. He retrieved the crumpled piece of paper that he placed in his coat pocket the evening before and straightened it out. He took a seat on his sofa and began to think who it could be or what it could mean, but he had no clues. His thought process was cut short when he heard a sharp beeping noise coming from outside. He checked his watch to see it was gone seven A.M. and Geoffrey was waiting for him outside. He sprang to his feet, grabbed his wallet and watch from the sideboard in the hallway, threw his coat over his shoulders before stuffing the letter into the inside pocket. He quickly slid on his shoes and rapidly did up the laces and left his home. He was greeted by a large grin from Geoffrey "you're late!" Geoffrey said sarcastically "I've always wanted to say that to you. No coffee this morning?" Geoffrey asked

"I was running late and didn't have time to make one"

"I'll get you one on the way" Geoffrey said before applying pressure to the accelerator. Steven's eyes remained fixed out the window as he was deep in thought. He reached into his pocket and felt the crumpled letter before saying "that sounds nice."

Steven spent the journey deep in thought, even the out of tune singing from Geoffrey could not distract him from his own mind.

They entered the precinct and went to their respective desks; Steven discarded the finished takeaway coffee cup Geoffrey had bought for him on the way. Geoffrey gave a big wave to the captain, who was always in before everyone else, and sat down. The captain appeared at the door of his office "detective Cooper, can I speak with you please?" Steven got up and walked round his desk and into his captain's office, he could not help but notice how tall the captain was standing behind his desk. This immaculately uniformed man with a thick goatee, short black hair and deep brown eyes.

"you wanted to see me captain Luther?" asked Steven

"yes, close the door", Steven obliged and took a seat in front of the desk. "Firstly, I'd like to take the opportunity to congratulate you on winning the 'employee of the year' award, being voted for by your colleagues is a huge honour" Steven blushed and smiled. "You deserve it for tolerating Osbourne for three years" the captain said with a smirk.

"Geoffrey may have his flaws but he's a good man and he's loyal. I wouldn't be sitting her today if it weren't for him."

"I know you wouldn't, but don't forget who put you two together all those years ago" said Captain Luther with a hint of boastfulness. "He has got a lot to learn from you though Steven"

"and I from him" returned Steven.

"Ha, always so modest" chimed captain Luther, "now, the reason I called you in here was to discuss the two open murder cases you have, any revelations?"

"No new leads yet, Geoffrey is on to the lab techs, as we speak. Video footage from the M&T lighting store proved futile, picture was distorted, and the suspect was well covered from view." Steven delivered "is there anything that links to two cases?" asked captain Luther as his tone lowered.

"Other than the fact both victims had high blood alcohol levels and were murdered in the early hours of the morning" Steven articulated.

"Well I'm getting some pressure from the higher ups about this, if any new info comes to light please tell me" captain Luther sympathised.

Steven thought about the note that had been left for him before saying "I will captain."

Steven exited the well organised office to see Geoffrey finishing up a phone call at his desk. He slowly walked over, as Geoffrey put the phone down "that was the crime lab, Mr Johnson, that's the name of the person found dead in the Highstreet, has no known next of kin."

"Right, I need you to look back through that footage and try to trace the whereabouts of our suspect prior to the murder." Geoffrey gave a nod of acknowledgement as Steven walked back to his desk, sat and swivelled in his chair.

He pulled himself closer to his desk and leaned into his computer.

He opened the digitised case files he'd solved during his time as a detective at H.T.P.D the first case that caught his eye was a string of B and E's that he and Geoffrey had solved almost two years ago. The guilty man had targeted electrical goods stores in the eastern part the precincts territory. He achieved three immaculate robberies collecting tens of thousands of pounds in electrical equipment. However, he got greedy, and lazy, leaving DNA evidence at his fourth and final heist. Steven searched the assailants name in the database and found he was still serving time in Hightower penitentiary, he also had no know partners on this case. Also, he never murdered anyone, he did however injure a security guard that startled him, but that is a far stretch from murder, Steven thought.

Steven discarded that case and began researching another which attracted his attention. A woman who murdered her drunk husband after she had had enough of his domestic violence. She moved the body from the crime scene and dumped it nearby. Steven remembered she was put into a rehabilitation centre to help with her mental health. She also only committed one murder and was obviously provoked. It cannot be her, he thought as he scrolled a little further. Suddenly a mugshot entered the screen which caused his index finger to stop rolling over his mouse. The picture was of a tanned Caucasian man, with long greyish black hair, a weathered face and a thin goatee framing his jaw. "Ivan Radzianko" Steven mumbled to himself as he slumped back in his chair, I remember that case all too well.

The morning was still, there was a hush among the swat team that was about infiltrate the den of Radzianko's drug operation. "On my mark" Steven said confidently as he raised his right hand which had three erect fingers. One by one he lowered a finger counting down "three...two...one move, move, move!" he shouted. As he did the swat team broke down the door of the hideout and rapidly began entering, Steven followed with his gun raised to eye level and the shouts of get down echoing around the warehouse. "Make sure we get Radzianko" yelled Steven as people began fleeing the scene like jackrabbits. Steven placed three shots into the chest of a man who was steam training towards him. He took cover behind a work bench, "where is he" he called in the deafening sound of gunfire. Surely enough Radzianko appeared from an upstairs office with a loaded AK47 firing shots into the air and at various members of the swat team. Steven looked up over the bench to see Radzianko in a black suit, cigar in mouth and clad with jewellery, running down the steel staircase. "There he is" bellowed Steven "don't let him escape." Radzianko hurdled the handrail at the bottom of the stairs and began to bolt for the back exit. Steven instinctively took off from his cover and began to peruse him, luckily dodging flying bullets which filled the room. He caught up to Radzianko who was having trouble unlocking the fire exit. "Give it up Ivan, it's the end of the line" Steven screamed "you think you've won" Radzianko responded in a thick Russian accent. "But you will never win" Radzianko began to raise his weapon, before he could take aim Steven released a swift shot into Ivan's right thigh, causing him to scream in agony. He dropped his weapon and Steven ran towards him and swiftly manacled the tall broad-shouldered man and took him back to the police station.

Steven was greeted at the precinct by a uniformed officer, "look in the holding cell" she said nodding her head towards the back-left corner of the room. Steven looked over to see a young man around sixteen years of age sitting with his arms folded in an upright position in the dimly lit cell. He turned to look at steven with a face like thunder, his dark brown eyes and shaven head accompanied his demeaner.

"Is that who I think it is?" asked steven

"yep, picked him up just outside of Radzianko's warehouse."

"That's great news" Steven mumbled as he headed down a thin corridor to begin his questioning.

Steven accompanied Radzianko in the interrogation room, not before letting him stew for an hour or two. He placed a solitary piece of paper on the desk as he took a seat on the metal chair opposite the steely eyed criminal, "let me guess, not going to talk" Steven asked as Radzianko stared blankly at the detective. "Ok I'll do the talking; your synthetic LSD has swept across Hightower like wildfire. The cause of hundreds of deaths and the influence of an increase in drug related crimes, stretching the H.T.P.D thin. Multiple accounts of murder, battery and money laundering"

"You can't tie me to any of those" Radzianko said calmly.

"we have eyewitnesses placing you at numerous scenes"

"are these eyewitnesses by chance convicted criminals themselves, testifying against me in return for a lifeline?" Ivan replied whilst smirking

"you're right were going to need a confession from you."

"And what makes you think I'll confess" asked Radzianko as he leaned in closer

"does the name Dimitri ring a bell?"

Radzianko widened his eyes before coolly saying "where is he?"

"in the frantic environment you thought your son had escaped like you planned. That is why you took so long to leave your office; you were helping your son out the first-floor window."

"Where is he?!" yelled Radzianko again

"he was picked up by a patrol car on the outskirts of your hideout, but don't worry he's safe with us."

"If you lay a finger on him, I'll"

"you'll what" Steven interrupted; Ivan slumped back into his chair. "Because he was caught fleeing a crime scene, he can be tried as an accessory to the crimes that were taking place and believe me there were a lot. Production and distribution of illegal narcotics, possession of unlicensed firearms shall I go on?" asked Steven rhetorically.

"He's a child" cried Radzianko

"and he'll be tried as such, but he will still spend time in a juvenile recreation facility, five maybe ten years, I know he's a bright kid, he wants to go to university to study chemistry doesn't he? How is he going to do that if he behind bars? and even when he is freed, I'll make damn sure he's not released into your custody!". Steven slid the typed letter across the steel table, "Sign on that line and I'll personally make sure he doesn't see the inside of a jail cell."

Steven sat back up in his chair and searched Radzianko's name in his computers data base, just as he thought he was still serving his thirty-five years in a high security prison in capital city, thirty miles north of Hightower. That is good news he thought as Geoffrey appeared at Stevens desk.

"The Radzianko case, that's the first one we worked together, and the case I saved your life" Geoffrey reminded Steven.

"Yes, thank you Geoffrey"

"I told you I won't let you forget it, anyway, I've got a few possible locations Mr Johnson could have been murdered, want to check them out?"

Steven closed the data base he was searching and pulled his coat of the back of his office chair "yeah, let's go."

Chapter six:

In Pursuit

The detectives exited the building and entered their car, they set out for the location that Geoffrey had earmarked as the most probable murder scene.

"Why do you think this is the most likely location?" asked Steven

"it's well-hidden, no security cameras and little foot traffic. It's also within walking distance of M&T lighting, which is a big plus if you have to carry a body whilst walking."

"Sounds good to me" Steven answered.

"Hey, that 'Genesis gardens' is coming along nicely" Geoffrey noticed as the pair passed the construction site of the attraction, "When's opening night?"

"Well the gardens open to the public next Saturday but our tickets are for next

Wednesday night. Claire is really looking forward to it, she loves flowers and botanicals and seeing her smile makes me happy."

Geoffrey rolled his eyes "too much information" he said as he pulled the car up to the possible murder location. The two detectives were now stood in front of M&T lighting, where the body was found.

"Where are we going?" asked Steven

"Follow me" Geoffrey began walking in the direction the suspicious man was seen carrying the deceased Mr Johnson. There was a small side passage located between a Geology store, selling geodes and other mineral based naturals, and a local gym, one of many located around the city of Hightower. "Right through here, between a rock and a hard place" Geoffrey quipped as he and Steven began walking down the narrow walkway. They arrived at the end to see large bins and rubbish bags filled the back of the stores. Steven and Geoffrey began looking around for clues, the smell of mouldy waste filled the air which caused Geoffrey to cover his nose with his sleeve. The buildings blocked the sunlight from reaching the area, and the only visible people were the ones walking the Highstreet, past the entrance to the shadowy passage, although, the hustle and bustle of the city was ever present. Geoffrey spotted a collection of brown cardboard boxes laid out behind one of the large bins. "Over here" he yelled as he gestured Steven over, "I'm willing to bet that this is another location that Mr Johnson liked to sleep"

Steven knelt closer to the crumpled boxes to gain a better view "looks like there was a sign of a struggle, or someone pushed this bin over the bed of boxes, either way we need more information. You head into the gym and see if anyone saw anything and I'll do the same in the geology shop." The pair walked back down the darkened walkway and separated towards their tasks.

Steven entered the Geology shop and walked to the counter, which was manned by an old, grey, be speckled gentleman handling a dark green emerald geode.

"How can I help you?" he asked

"I'm detective Cooper" Steven responded as he pulled his ID from his waist "we're investigating a Mr Johnson, he's the homeless man who frequents this high street. We have reason to believe he sometimes slept in the bin area round back?"

"umm yes, I saw him around from time to time but never spoke to him. I know that he liked to sleep out the back, but I thought he wasn't harming anyone, so I let him do it. May I ask what it's about?"

"Mr Johnson was found dead in M&T lighting, two stores down the way."

"Oh my, I know he liked to sleep in the alcove of the building, I even threw him some of my change from time to time."

"Do you have security cameras?" asked Steven

"no, sorry I have an alarm system but no security cameras."

"Can you think of anything that may help us with our investigation?"

"Not at the moment" the clerk shrugged,

"if you do please contact us" Steven handed the gentleman a card with his contact information printed on the front before leaving the store.

As Steven left, he noticed a tall figure standing in the alleyway across the street. Dressed in a long black coat and an equally dark hat, the man caught Stevens gaze before bolting. Steven began pursuit he halted two cars as he crossed the street, one almost hitting him, before yelling "police, stop!" He brushed his shoulder on the wall of the narrow alleyway as he entered it. He reached where the man was standing, he looked to the left and saw another thin passage where the man had just turned right, out of his view. He pushed off the sidewall to gain extra speed as he continued his pursuit, he hurdled a discarded black rubbish bag before slipping on a puddle that had formed on the other side of the abandoned waste. He regained his footing turned right into a bricked corridor which opened into a busy sun kissed road. He reached the exit and hurriedly looked from left to right, either the man had vanished, or he couldn't see him through the thick crowd of citizens.

Suddenly Steven heard heavy breathing coming from behind him, he quickly swivelled as he placed his hand on his holstered gun.

"whoa, it's me" gasped Geoffrey as he raised his hands with his palms facing towards Steven. "why were you running?"

"I saw someone that was wearing the same coat the man was wearing in the video footage. When he saw me, he made a break for it, but I lost him" He said clutching his leg.

"You ok?"

"Yeah, I slipped whilst chasing the suspect" Steven raised his trouser leg to reveal a large, bloody graze starting at the midpoint of his calf and extending past the kneecap.

"You need to get that checked out"

"honesty its fine" Steven responded as he checked his watch, "Just drop me home."

The pair returned to the squad car and headed for Stevens family home. Steven, still fastening his leg with his hand.

"Didn't you say Olivia was a nurse?" asked Steven.

"No, how did you... you looked her up online didn't you?"

"I was interested, and I wasn't going to get any information out of you, she's really pretty."

"Yeah, I know she is, it's just relationships scare me, I don't know if I will ever feel like I'm ready to settle down" Geoffrey sighed

"Don't be stupid Geoffrey, you're young you've got plenty of time to find someone, settle down and start a family. Look at me, I was nowhere near being a family man at your age." Steven was forty-two years of age and Geoffrey was twelve years his junior.

The pair pulled up outside Steven's home, said their goodbyes and parted ways. Steven entered his house, grappling his thigh as he walked up the stairs, He hadn't heard his wife sneak up behind him. "What have you done" she said caringly

"I slipped on an uneven sidewalk" Steven lied "but it's fine."

"Are you going to be alright for date night?"

"I wouldn't miss it for the world."

Every Tuesday night Steven and Claire Cooper spent their evening at 'The Lychee Palace', a small well-lit Thai restaurant, decorated with oriental artwork. This was the scene of their first date over five years ago, since the relationship started the pair hadn't missed a Tuesday date night. Both Steven and Claire enjoyed these evenings as it was a chance to reflect on the love, they had for one another. Their reservation was always booked for seven thirty, the owner of the restaurant knew the Coopers very well as she greeted them at the restaurant every Tuesday night, and tonight was no different.

"Let me guess, table for two" she chuckled as the Coopers waited at the front of the restaurant to be seated. The pair smiled and they were shown to their seats. Steven pulled the chair out for his wife to sit before he took his own seat. "Any drinks?" asked the owner, who had shown them to their table "I'll have a medium Shiraz" requested Claire.

"Very good, and for you sir?" the owner asked as she moved her gaze from Claire to Steven.

"umm water's fine" he answered, the lady left, not before lighting the white candle in the middle of the table. Steven could not help but notice how lively the restaurant was tonight, "it is packed in here" he said to his wife in amongst the chatter and hub bub of the eatery.

Claire looked around to confirm Stevens comment "it really is" she answered, "it's nice to see them doing so well, oh, I got my teaching plan for next year."

"Oh yeah, anything interesting?" Steven asked

"there's a part on revolutions like the Russian, French and reformation of the English church that I am fascinated by" Claire responded eagerly. Steven just stared at his wife "what?" she asked

"I just love how passionate you get about things" Claire smiled back at her husband.

A waiter returned with their drinks order and asked, "what can I get for you?"

"I'll have the Thai green curry please" responded Steven.

"And I'll have the vegetable stir fry" followed Claire

"perfect" the waiter replied as he took the menus from their table. Steven raised his hand above the tabletop, reached out and placed it on top of Claire's hand which was resting on the table. He stared into Claire's bright blues eyes; the lights of the room sparkled off the pearl earrings she was wearing. "Are those the ones you mum left you?"

"yeah, she knew I loved them and when she passed, they were left to me" responded a teary-eyed Claire.

"They're beautiful, as are you" Claire blushed as the food was delivered.

"Do you remember when you asked me what my favourite film was, on our first date?" Claire asked

"yes, you said Casablanca."

"I did, and do you remember your response?"

"yes, I very awkwardly said 'here's looking at you kid', and I distinctly remember you laughing at me."

"Yeah, it was funny that's why I laughed, but I will always remember it because it was the first time you tried to be romantic and I knew you liked me... a lot."

"Well, looking at how things turned out I'd say you we're right about me liking you"

"I wouldn't have it any other way. Oh, before I forget I'm going out with a few of the teachers from work tomorrow night, so you'll need to sort out dinner for Lily."

"That's one way to ruin a moment" Steven quipped.

The pair enjoyed a lovely meal they paid the bill, leaving a large tip, as Steven always did, collected their coats and left the restaurant. Steven detoured on the way home heading past the new botanical gardens. He pulled up facing the car towards the building, the vehicle was lit from the green lights emanating from the Genesis gardens.

"I can't wait" Claire said excitedly

"not long, just over a week to go" Steven looked towards Claire and she met his gaze. Their faces illuminated by the green flood lights, they moved in closer and their lips locked.

Chapter Seven:

Without a trace

The next morning, Steven awoke at his usual time; he'd slept far better than he had the night before. He followed his morning ritual, shower, clothes, coffee, wallet, phone, keys, coat, before waiting at the end of his garden for Geoffrey to collect him. Twenty minutes past and Geoffrey still hadn't arrived, Steven looked at his watch repeatedly whilst sipping his almost finished coffee. Eventually a squad car turned round the corner of the end of the street, Steven rose from the relaxed position he had taken up on the wall, which framed his front garden. The squad car pulled up and Steven lazily opened the door and slumped into the car. "I thought I was going to have to walk again" Steven quipped

"one time that happened" responded Geoffrey "and you never let me forget it. Anyway, there's a reason why I'm late, and I think you're going to like it"

"why's that then?"

"After I dropped you home yesterday, I decided to head back to where you saw our suspect. I found a security camera in view of the alleyway where you lost sight of him."

"Really, did you find anything?" said an interested Steven

"I took the footage home and riffled through it. Here's the odd thing nobody leaves the opening of the passage before you and I arrive."

"What?"

"I know, odd right, so either you're seeing people that aren't there or the suspect never left the alley."

"I take it we're heading straight there?"

Geoffrey turned to Steven, the morning sun shining off the corner of his sunglasses, "obviously" Geoffrey sarcastically replied.

The two detectives arrived at the scene of the pursuit; they followed the thin bricked passages to where Steven had lost sight of the assailant.

"Watch the puddle!" Geoffrey laughed "wouldn't want you falling over again" Steven stared blankly at Geoffrey. "Just a joke, how is the leg?" Geoffrey asked

"It's fine" Steven responded whilst wincing.

The pair began to inspect the tall chasm-like passage, the sun had trouble lighting the floor of the alley due to the high buildings either side. The cobblestone ground was damp from the rainfall the night before, the smell of rotting waste filled the air. Steven walked to the exit and turned one-hundred and eighty degrees "look, up there" he called. Behind Geoffrey and two feet above him was a steel ladder leading to the top of the high-rises. "You think he went up there" Geoffrey queried

"hop on the bin to your left and reach over."

Geoffrey obliged, he clumsily crawled onto the large waste unit, leant over and grasped the bottom rung of the ladder. He pulled himself up a few more rungs before turning round and looking at Steven "why am I doing this and not you?" he asked. Steven pointed to his leg as Geoffrey rolled his eyes and began ascending.

Geoffrey reached the top of the ladder and looked across the vast, flat roofed apartment buildings. Steam was slowly appearing from an extract system to his left, he took a panoramic view, taking in the tall structures of Hightower. The morning sun was starting to warm up and was becoming bright, Geoffrey could see for miles. "See anything" yelled Steven, the sound of his voice just reaching Geoffrey's ears. He turned back and looked down towards his partner whilst gesturing a thumbs down motion with his right hand. He began his decent, he dropped from the bottom rung onto the uneven floor and gathered his balance. "If he did climb up there, he could have gone any direction" Geoffrey informed Steven.

"Well, I lost sight of him when I slipped, I assumed he ran to the end of the alleyway, but the security footage suggests he did not. Let's head back to the precinct." If the suspect was willing to go to that much effort to avoid him, he must be involved in some way, Steven thought to himself.

They headed back to the squad car and drove to the precinct, "It's Lily's birthday tomorrow isn't it?" asked Geoffrey "what have you got her?"

"She's been going on about a Miss Millicent toy set, apparently all the girls at school have got it"

"how old is she going to be?"

"Twelve" responded Steven "we're also throwing a birthday party on Saturday, lots of screaming kids, unhealthy food and party games, you're more than welcome to come."

"Sounds fun" Geoffrey responded sarcastically, "but I'll be there, if you don't mind me asking, will Lily's real dad be there? I know you've said in the past how she used to see him often, then suddenly they stopped seeing each other."

"I don't think he will be there; Lily hasn't seen him in three years, and he wasn't the best of husbands to Claire. She told me he used to drink a lot and when he did, he got violent, I think Claire was relieved when he and Lily stopped contact, why do you ask?"

"No reason, just making conversation, want some lunch?"

Once back at the precinct, Steven and Geoffrey headed to the break room with the turkey sandwiches they had acquired on the way. Sitting on the worn, blue sofa in amongst the smell of burnt coffee grounds they began to chat. "How's things going with Olivia?" questioned Steven

"who?"

"The girl you've been seeing"

"why do you keep asking?"

"I'm interested, and Claire keep going on about double dating."

"whoa, we are nowhere near double dating position yet. I'm not ever sure things will last; I haven't seen her in over a week."

"It will happen you just need to put yourself out there, you might get your heart broken, but you will never find what you want unless you do."

"You're right... I guess"

"I usually am" smirked Steven as he finished his turkey sandwich, threw the wrapper into the bin across the room and sipped the last of his coffee.

Steven returned to his office space, he sat down, just as he did, a uniformed officer tapped him on the shoulder. "The parents of Miss Willow are here to see you" said the officer, Steven looked past the officer to see a suited man with short black hair and stubbled face. He looked agitated almost annoyed, next to him was a blonde short haired woman wearing blue jeans and a white blouse. She had long pink nails and her wrists and fingers were clad with jewellery. "Ok, thank you" responded Steven, he rose from his seat and marched to where the couple were seated. "Hi, I'm detective Cooper" Steven said whilst holding out his hand

"Simon and Angela Willow" responded the man as he grasped Steven's outstretched palm and shook it. "We're here to find out more information about our daughters' case"

"follow me" Steven guided the pair to an empty interrogation room, for privacy, and they all took their seats. "Firstly, I'd like to say just how sorry I am for your loss, I can't imagine what you're going through."

"Thank you" responded Angela as a tear trickled down her face "how is the case going, do you have any leads?"

"we don't have any leads yet, but my partner and I are investigating every avenue. I can promise you we are doing all we can, but these things take time"

"nothing!" yelled an aggravated Mr Willow "my daughter was found dead six days ago and you're telling me you have no idea who could've done it."

"please calm down Mr Willow, like I said before we are following every possible option, but these things take time" reiterated Steven. "If you would allow me, I'd like to ask you some questions?"

"sure" responded a teary-eyed Mrs Willow.

"When was the last time you saw your daughter?"

"at Christmas she travelled up to Capital city to stay with us during the festive period."

"that was six months ago, did you not see your daughter often?"

"well, life is busy, as you know."

"Your daughters roommate Mr Freeman said you didn't see eye to eye, something to do with her drinking or party life?"

Mr Willow sat back in his chair and crossed his arms, Steven could see that question struck a nerve.

"She did like a drink and sometimes it got the better of her, we thought that once she graduated University, she would leave the drinking and party life behind, but if anything, it got worse."

"What do you mean it got worse?"

"she went out almost every night with friends, we couldn't go a week without the police on our doorstep bringing her home or telling us she had been arrested. When she decided to move down to Hightower with Paul (Mr Freeman) we were somewhat relieved."

"This is useless" screamed Mr Willow "sitting in here questioning us on how much we love our daughter is not going to find her killer!"

"I understand your frustration" Steven said calmly "but all this information is important to finding the person who did this."

"I don't see how" bellowed Mr Willow as he stood up and banged the desk, "come on dear were leaving" he grabbed his wife and pulled her from her seat. He swung open the door to the interrogation room and marched out of the precinct. Steven took a moment before getting up, pushing the chairs under the table and leaving the room as he closed the door behind him.

He walked back into the bullpen to see Geoffrey sheepishly looking over his shoulder. "Whoever that was he looked pissed"

"that was Mr and Mrs Willow, they were here to find out how the investigation was going"

"oh... right."

Steven knew that Geoffrey understood how the conversation went without having to tell him about it.

Chapter Eight:
Secrets

The rest of the workday dragged, Steven spent his time chasing cold leads, phoning people to confirm alibis and wracking his brain over who could've left him the note. All of which proved uneventful, by five o'clock Steven had had enough, he gathered his belongings and the pair headed home.

"I'm really starting to worry we're not going to find our murderer on either of these cases" Geoffrey said as he started the engine of the squad car.

"We just need to keep working these cases and I'm sure new information will show up, we just need to be patient."

"Do you think the cases can are connected?" Geoffrey queried "if they are, I don't see how, the MO is slightly different on both, the first choked and stabbed and the second was just strangled. Killers don't just mix it up like that. The victims both abused alcohol but that doesn't narrow it down, and both people didn't know each other as far as I can see. Do you think their linked?"

"there is maybe something in the fact that both have gone cold, little evidence, no DNA left at either scene and no witnesses or useful footage. Either that's a coincidence or we have a clever individual on our hands."

"Perhaps your right Geoffrey"

"now that's something you don't say often."

Geoffrey halted the car outside the Coopers family home, Steven exited the vehicle, he was met halfway up the path to his front door by his wife. She was wearing light blue jeans and a frilly black top, she had her hair up in a bun, which pronounced the golden hooped earrings she was modelling. Her perfect smile was framed by her dark red lipstick, Steven's loving trance was disturbed by a wolf whistle coming from behind him, he turned to hear Geffrey yell. "Looking foxy Mrs Cooper" followed by a wink

"go home Geoffrey" called Steven exasperatedly, Geoffrey obliged and sped off. Steven turned to Claire "where are you going" he asked

"I told you, I'm going out for drinks with some colleagues from work."

"when did you tell me?"

"at dinner last night"

"oh yeah I remember, you ruined the moment we we're having by telling me"

Claire rolled her eyes before kissing Steven on the lips. A black town car pulled up outside their residence, she opened the passenger side door and hoped in. Steven blew her a kiss and waved her off, Steven turned back towards his home and walked the remainder of the path to him house. He was greeted but an excited Lily "just you and me tonight" she screamed as

Steven knelt to hug her, dropping his keys in the process.

"I know, what do you want to do?"

"I want to play with my toys, watch TV, eat sweets."

"whoa, slow down I can do all of that except the sweets. You need to sleep well tonight; do you know why"

"co'z it's my birthday tomorrow!" Lily screamed as Steven winced.

"It is but first we need to sort out dinner"

The pair enjoyed an evening of board games, Steven always losing, eating takeaway pizza, and watching old films. As Steven sat on the sofa with Lily fast asleep in his arms, he brushed her hair from her face, and grinned. "I truly am lucky to have what I have" he thought, the sound of keys rattling at the door distracted him from his epiphany. Claire entered to see that pair cozied up on the sofa together, and Casablanca on the television. "I told her it was your favourite, she insisted we watch it, apparently she's not the biggest fan" Steven said referencing Lily's tranquil state. Claire walked over and leaned in closer to Steven and whispered "here's looking at you kid" before kissing him passionately on the lips and heading upstairs to bed. Steven reached for the remote and switched off the television set, he slowly stood up as to not wake lily before picking her up, still sleeping, and carrying her to her bedroom. He placed her on her bed, kissed her on the cheek and left the room, remembering to leave to door slightly ajar because Lily didn't like the dark. He walked across the landing to his bedroom, he entered holding his back "I really need to stop picking her up, it gives my back grief." Claire entered the room from the on-suite bathroom, wearing a black lace lingerie set and a pair of tight stockings "what was that about your back" she asked whilst walking to the bed and taking a seat. Steven's eyes were bulging from his head as he hurriedly kicked off his slippers and whipped of his t-shirt, revealing his hairy chest, "nothing, absolutely nothing" he responded powerwalking towards his beautiful wife.

Steven woke the next day, before his alarm, he rolled over to look at his still sleeping wife and couldn't help but smile. He stretched his arms above his head, extended his legs and rolled out the side of the bed. Once he prepared himself for work in his usual fashion, he left the house and waited at the end of his front garden, sipping his piping hot coffee. Steven had drunk half of his coffee before Geoffrey arrived, the car pulled up in front of him and he slid in. "You really need to work on you time management skills" Steven joked

"hey, I'm so inconsistent that I'm consistent" returned Geoffrey as he found the biting point and pulled away from Stevens home.

"I've got a good feeling about today" Steven smiled

"you're in a good mood."

"I just had a really good night's sleep last night"

Geoffrey looked over at Steven with a large, insinuating grin "you got some last night, didn't you?"

"A gentleman never tells" smirked Steven.

The detectives arrived at the precinct and headed to their workstations, Steven collected all the information they had gathered on both cases and headed to an empty briefing room. He spent an hour or so organising and displaying the evidence on a white board, before collecting Geoffrey to come and assist him.

In the centre of the board they placed the victims from both cases (Miss Willow and Mr Johnson). Steven began placing string strands leading to evidence in the Miss Willow case as Geoffrey did the same with the Mr Johnson case. The strands lead to the murder weapon (the germanium pipe), the location of the murder (the alleyway at the end of forty second street), and known people of interest (Mr Freeman, The Willows, Miss Willow's colleagues and the wavy haired man). Geoffrey had achieved the same feat on the other side of the board, the stands leading to the cause of death (asphyxiation), location of murder (bin area behind the geology store/gym), the location the body was found (M&T lighting). The pair stepped back from their work and took a moment to comprehend it all. "What are you thinking?" asked Steven

"I'm thinking the longer I look at it the more complicated it becomes."

"There must be something were missing"

The thought process of the detectives was interrupted by an officer peering their head around the door of the briefing room. "A Mrs Angela Willow is here to see you"

"I'm not sure I've had enough coffee to deal with them this morning", quipped Steven as he took a deep breath

"Actually, it's just Mrs Willow her husband isn't here" responded the officer

Steven swivelled the board around, hiding the cases, showing a blank side of the board "can you send her in please."

Mrs Willow arrived in the briefing room with the two detectives. "Morning Mrs Willow" Steven said as he gestured to an empty chair behind a table at the front of the room. "This is detective Geoffrey Osbourne" Geoffrey nodded before adding "sorry for your loss."

"Thank you" said a nervous Mrs Willow quietly

"is Mr Willow not here with you today?" asked Steven.

"um… no he doesn't know I'm here." Steven looked at Geoffrey they both knew something was up "the reason he doesn't know I'm here is because what I'm about to tell you, he doesn't know". Steven and Geoffrey pulled up chairs in front of the grieving mother and sat down listening intently. "My daughter was attending an alcoholics anonymous program to help with her drinking problem, she told me at Christmas."

"Why didn't she tell her dad?" asked Steven

"as you saw from yesterday, he's not the easiest to talk to, Penelope feared opening up to her father. She was planning on going to these meetings for a while and hopefully overcoming her problem. She was excited to surprise her dad when that time came, but I guess that's irrelevant now."

"Do you know where these meetings took place?"

"I've never been there, but she did leave a card with an address on it when she visited over the holidays". Mrs Willow rummaged through her handbag and pulled out a business card, she handed it over to Steven. "Please find my daughter's killer" she asked sadly "I know our family doesn't seem close, but I love my daughter and I regret not spending more time with her". A solitary tear trickled down the face of Mrs Willow, Geoffrey reached into his pocket and revealed a tissue, handed it to the tearful mother as she wiped her cheek dry.

"We will do everything in our power Mrs Willow" added Geoffrey "I can promise you that."

Chapter Nine:

The Game

Mrs Willow left the police station in her distressed state accompanied by the uniformed officer that had shown her in. The two detectives collected their coats, wallets and keys and headed for the location printed on the card Mrs Willow had handed them. They entered the car and Geoffrey turned the key to start the engine, "twenty-one Crossgrove street" Steven said looking at the business card in his hand.

"That's not too far from where Mr Johnson was found dead"

"it's not, and I am hoping this is the clue we've been waiting for."

The pair arrived at the small building, a rec centre which held multiple groups and clubs, a notice board outside read. 'three – four P.M. after school club, four – five P.M. Zumba, five –

six P.M. roller disco, six – seven P.M. alcoholics anonymous'. "Looks like we're in the right place" said Geoffrey as the detectives entered the building. A small dimly lit foyer area, with little furnishings and a coffee table cluttered with old magazines greeted them. A modest front desk, which was being monitored by a tall, dark haired man with a short beard and big smile caught their attention. They walked over "I'm detective Steven Cooper and this is detective Geoffrey Osbourne" Steven said with his ID held aloft. "we're interested in the alcoholics anonymous club you hold every evening between six and seven P.M."

"well, there's plenty of room for new members" said the tall man behind the desk.

"Were not here to join" Steven returned "were here about a member, Miss Penelope Willow"

"ah, yes Miss Willow she's one of our newest members, haven't seen her in a few days though, is everything alright?"

"I'm sorry to say that Miss Willow was found dead on Friday morning" the man slumped into the chair behind him.

"That's such a shame, she had just started coming to these meetings and was really trying to get a grip on her habit."

"Did you know Miss Willow well?"

"as well as I knew the other members, I never saw her, or any of the other members outside of the meetings."

"And what is your roll here?"

"I'm operations manager, booking and organising events, I also run a few, the AA meetings included."

"Do you have a record of participants?"

"we have a logbook, we ask people to sign it so we know how many people are in the building, just to conform to fire safety regulations, however most wouldn't sign with their real name."

"Can we see the logbook?"

"Yeah sure just let me grab It" the man behind the desk swivelled round and opened the top drawer of the central filing cabinet behind him. He reached in and pulled out a black hardback book, he spun back around and placed it at the edge of the desk, nearest the detectives. Steven opened the book and turned the page back one week, he ran his finger past name after name, Mr Smith, miss mouse, Mrs J Mooney, Mr D Mendeleev, Mr Dennehy. "There" called Geoffrey, Steven stopped his finger from tracing and hovered it over the name of Miss Willow. "So, she came here the evening before she died"

"look a few names lower" returned Steven as he shifted his forefinger down the page. The name of one Mr Johnson was pencilled in "what are the chances that is our second victim." Steven rhetorically questioned Geoffrey, "what can you tell me about Mr Johnson?" Steven inquired.

"Just as much as I can tell you about Miss Willow, he's been coming here a short time, I believe he maybe homeless as he comes in the same clothes and unmistakable odour. But as for personal information I can't tell you anymore, the lack of personal questions is what brings people in."

"Thanks for your time" Steven replied, "can we get a copy of the logbook?". The man behind the desk took the book and photocopied the pages, which he handed to the detectives. They headed out of the building and back to their squad car.

"Looks like we found our link" said Steven as he and Geoffrey entered the squad car simultaneously "I told you something would come up", Geoffrey started the car.

"This suggests that our suspect attended these meetings, that's how he chose his victims, the problem is most of these names may be false."

"We will look into them when we get back to the precinct"

"ok, but first I need to stop off somewhere". Geoffrey turned onto a busy high street and pulled up outside a toy shop, he undid his seatbelt "back in a sec" he said as he hopped out the vehicle and entered the toy store. Steven sat waiting in the sun warmed vehicle for a few moments before Geoffrey re-emerged and threw himself back into the car. "Lily will like this won't she?" Geoffrey showed Steven a toy horse with customisable mane and tail.

"I'm sure she'll love it"

The pair left the high street and headed back to the precinct, they entered the bullpen, threw their coats onto their respective chairs. "I'll meet you in the briefing room" said Geoffrey as he headed towards the recently brewed pot of coffee. Steven took the photocopied logbook and set up a workstation in the room, just in front of the whiteboard they had decorated with case information. Geoffrey joined Steven in the room, carrying two piping hot cups of coffee, and sat next to Steven. "I've separated the logbook into piles, I think our best bet is to read through them and tally what names reappear and how many times."

"Hopefully, that can lead to something" Geoffrey replied as he burnt his tongue by sipping on his coffee.

The pair sat for over an hour riffling through pages and tallying names, their progress was interrupted by the captain entering the room. The detectives looked up at the towering captain, "Raymond"

"please don't call me by my first name detective Osbourne" responded captain Luther.

"What's up captain?" asked Steven

"just coming to check up on your cases, how's it going?"

"they went cold, but some new information has put us onto a different path, so fingers crossed" answered Steven.

"That's good news, do you mind If I chat with you in my office Steven?" Steven looked at Geoffrey and Geoffrey reflected the motion.

"Of course," Steven rose from his seat and followed captain Luther into his office.

"Close the door", Steven did so and sat in front of the captain's desk, Captain Luther sat in his larger chair on the opposite side before letting out an audible sigh.

"I'm getting a lot of grief from the commissioner about those cases Steven, probably because we've got the 'Genesis gardens' opening soon, which is going to bring in a lot of activity to Hightower, mostly from Capital city, and having a serial killer on the lose is not good publicity."

"I wouldn't call two murders that have no obvious links the work of a serial killer captain" argued Steven.

"Well, officer Carmichael called in a reported murder this morning, forensics have been on the case and detective Smith was first on the scene",

"and you think it's related to the two open cases Geoffrey and I have been working?"

"Yes" responded the captain sullenly

"whys that, was the victim a recovering alcoholic, are they a relation of our previous victims, does the M.O. match?"

"No, none of those"

"well, what's the connection then" asked an impatient Steven. The captain reached into his top right-hand drawer, pulled a clear plastic bag with a single, bloody, piece of paper sealed inside. He slapped it on the desk and slid it towards Steven.

"you!" he said seriously.

Steven leant forward in his chair to see written on the paper, 'Found the Link? Detective Cooper'.

Chapter ten:

Highs and Lows

Steven slumped back into his chair, his face was as white as a ghost, his heart sunk. He thought back to the first letter, from what he could remember the writing seemed to match.

"Do you know anything about this? Asked Captain Luther

"no, I have no clue who it could be."

"they seem to know who you are detective, have you received any other notes like this?" Steven took a moment before replying.

"No"

"Ok, I've asked detective Smith to transfer the case over to you and Geoffrey, do you think you can handle this?"

"Yes captain, if anything it makes me want to catch the person even more"

"I'll get detective Smith to give you everything he's gathered on the case, and Steven look after yourself, if you ever need anything you know where my office is."

"Thanks captain" Steven slowly stood up and took the evidence from the captain's desk

"one more thing captain, what was the name of the victim?"

"Mr Mark Jones"

"thank you" Steven exited the office and headed straight for the briefing room where Geoffrey was still working his way through the logbook. "typical, now you show up just as I've finished both piles. What's the matter you look like you've seen a ghost?" Steven placed the bagged evidence onto the table in front of Geoffrey "what's this?" Geoffrey questioned as he picked up the bag and took a good look. He lowered the bag from his face to reveal a dropped jaw and wide-open eyes. "I'm speechless, where was this found? who is it? Do you know them?"

"I can't answer any of those questions, just when I thought we we're making progress on these cases, more questions arise."

"Where shall we start?" asked Geoffrey

"Captain said the name of the victim was Mark Jones, does that name appear in the logbook."

"Let's see Jones… Jones… Jones, nobody called Jones, the names that appear most often are Miss Willow, Mr Mendeleev, Miss James, Mrs Li, Mr Dennehy and Dr Moore, but my guess is that they're not a real doctor."

"Right, we need to check out the crime scene"

"Hold on its four o'clock, you need to get home its Lily's birthday you wouldn't want to be late."

"But we need to work the case"

"I'll work the case for the time being, I'll drop you home, then come back get the information from Smithy and go and secure the crime scene, then tomorrow morning we'll head over there first thing and catch this son of a bitch, sound like a plan?"

"Yeah, sounds good cheers Geoffrey"

"hey, what are partners for"

The two detectives headed for the car and subsequently Steven's home. "It's odd how the killer left you a note on the third victim, he's not giving you much of a chance" Geoffrey said quizzically.

"Yeah that is odd" Steven mumbled as the pair drove away from the precinct.

"I have to admit I'm a little jealous that you've got a nemesis?" joked Geoffrey as he tried to lighten the serious mood.

"Give it time, I'm sure you'll have one soon enough"

"can you think of anyone who it can be?"

"I honestly can't, I've been a detective for fifteen years, I've put a lot of people away not to mention the lives it's affected by putting those people away."

"Yeah right, do me a favour tonight" Geoffrey asked, Steven looked up from his thoughtful state. "Enjoy your evening, try to not think about this and celebrate Lily's birthday, I know what you're like, you have trouble shutting off."

"Yeah, I'll try"

Geoffrey pulled the car up to Steven's home, Steven exited, walked the path of his front garden, opened his front door and was greeted by a screaming and excited Lily.

"Happy birthday" Yelled Steven

"thank you" Lily replied whilst hugging Steven around the waist. Steven removed his coat and place it on the rack, he walked into the living room to see a pile of brightly wrapped presents by the tv.

"Look at all those, someone must love you", Lily gave out a huge grin aimed at Steven as Claire entered the room from the kitchen. "Hi darling" she said, Steven walked towards his wife kissed her on the cheek and turned back to Lily.

"I'm going to get changed, when I get back, we can open presents, how does that sound?"

"yeah". Steven headed upstairs and removed his, tie, white shirt and navy trousers and threw on a pair of grey jogging bottoms and a white t-shirt. He slipped on his blue slippers and quickly jogged back downstairs. He joined Claire who was sitting on the sofa with a cup of tea in her hands "there's one for you on the table" she said gesturing towards the glass coffee table in the middle of the room.

"Can I start" cried Lily

"yes, go on" Claire responded

Lily grabbed present after present, ripping the colourful wrapping paper from the concealed gifts. She let out an eek after she realised what each present was as Steven and Claire winced whilst trying to maintain a smile.

She picked up a large cubed gift, wrapped in pink, Lily's favourite colour, and purple wrapping paper. A big, sparkly bow completed the design, "who is it from?" asked Claire. Lily lifted the colour coordinated tag that hung from the side of the present and turned it round.

"To Lily, hope your birthday is as special as you are, lots of love Mummy and Daddy". She looked up and gave her biggest smile of the evening before frantically ripping at the material to see what was hidden beneath. "OH MY GOD!" she yelled

"what is it?" asked Steven

"it's a Miss Millicent doll, thank you so much, I love it." Lily jumped up and ran towards the sofa before leaping onto her parents "I love you" she said whilst in a medley on the sofa, both Steven and Claire gripped her tightly. Lily returned to the floor and noticed one last unopened gift lying under the mound of discarded wrapping paper. She threw the gift wrap aside, lifted the present and read the tag "To Lily, love you, Alex" who's Alex she asked. "He's a friend" returned Claire as her eyes shifted towards Steven, Steven knew who Alex was, he was Claire's previous husband and the Father of Lily. His cheerful expression dropped as Claire said "we will talk about it later" before putting her hand on Stevens thigh, Lily opened the present to find a small, fluffy toy bunny rabbit she used to play with as a kid. She gave it a hug and placed it with the collection of other presents she had received that evening.

"Are you hungry?" Claire asked Lily as she could still see Steven deep in thought

"yeah" she cried.

"I've made your favourite, lasagne"

"yay" Lily ran to the kitchen and took her seat at the dinner table; Claire followed and removed the hot dish from the oven. Steven stayed seated in the living room for a few moments before slowly joining his family in the kitchen. He took his place at the table, a sullen look was plastered on his face, Claire served the food to Lily, and a vegetarian version for herself. When she walked behind Steven, she placed her arms around his shoulders and kissed him on the cheek "I love you" she whispered. Steven put his hand on hers and smiled, the dinner was a stark contrast between Lily's sheer enjoyment and Stevens expressionless state. Lily finished her dinner and ran from the table to play with her newly acquired toys. "You've not eaten your salad" called Claire, but Lily pretended not the hear her. "Have you finished dear?" Claire asked Steven, he nodded his head even though his plate was still half full, "you've not eaten much" Claire noticed.

"Big lunch" Steven responded, he'd skipped lunch that day, but he didn't have much of an appetite, he was too distracted to eat.

The evening went by quickly, Lily tired herself out by playing with her gifts whist Claire and Steven watched and joined in occasionally. Around seven-thirty P.M. Claire headed to the kitchen and returned with a small chocolate birthday cake, holding up twelve lit, pink candles. She flicked the light switch to darken the room as she and Steven began to sing happy birthday. Claire slowly walked over to Lily as they sang the last line, she lowered the cake down to Lily's level as she hastily blew out the candles. "Who wants cake?" Claire asked

"me!" screamed Lily

Steven remained quiet whilst Claire served Lily cake, he didn't change until Claire sent Lily to bed and kissed her goodnight. Lily ran upstairs, her Miss Millicent doll in hand, and got ready to go to sleep. "I'm sorry I didn't tell you about the gift from Alex" Claire said apologetically. "He popped round out of the blue Monday afternoon and handed me the present."

"Are you still keeping in touch with him?"

"god no, I haven't seen him in over three years"

"what and now suddenly he wants to be part of Lily's life again, it doesn't add up."

"He begged me to let him see her, obviously I said no, but I agreed to let her open his present."

"From what you've told me, he wasn't a good husband to you Claire, I don't think he should be allowed to see her. Especially since it's been so long"

"I agree but it's not easy saying no when he's standing at the door pleading with me, I had to compromise."

"But that's the last you see of him" Steven said defiantly

"don't tell me what I can and can't do Steven"

"oh, so you want to spend time with your ex-husband and encourage him to be part of Lily's life."

"You're being irrational, I'm going to bed, I'll talk to you when you've come to your senses" Claire stormed upstairs, stomping on each step as she did. Steven walked to the small cupboard below the stairs and collected a large duvet and a pair of un-sheeted pillows and tossed them onto the sofa. He slumped across the chair with his head propped up by one arm and his feet extending beyond the other. Lying with his eyes wide and fixed on a solitary point on the ceiling he thought about how the day had gone from bad to worse.

Chapter Eleven:
The Third Victim

Steven woke from his uncomfortable slumber, he sat up aided by the arm of the sofa. He stretched out his spine and his stiff neck before rubbing his eyes and shuffling off. He packed away the sleeping materials he'd collected from under the stairs the night before, he didn't want Lily to see as she would know something was wrong. He walked upstairs and into his bedroom, he tip toed past his sleeping wife and into the on-suite bathroom to prepare himself for his workday. He dressed himself and crept back downstairs, he headed straight to the kitchen to make himself a coffee, he went and collected his keys and wallet from the sideboard and grabbed his coat from the rack and tucked it under his arm. He left his house to wait at the perimeter for Geoffrey to arrive, sure enough the unmistakable squad car turned the corner of the road and pulled up in front of

Steven. He Joined his partner in the vehicle and was greeted by a cheerful "morning" as he pulled away

"Morning Geoffrey" replied Steven as he tried to stifle a yawn.

"Late night was it? See any action?" Geoffrey laughed

"no, Claire and I had an argument and I ended up sleeping on the sofa, I didn't get a good night's sleep at all" Steven said rubbing the back of his neck.

"I told you to forget about work and enjoy the evening, I would handle the case"

"I did, and we were having a great evening until Claire told me her ex-husband had visited and left a present for Lily."

"Wait I thought Lily hadn't seen her dad in years, what is he doing showing up randomly?"

"that's what I thought, but when I confronted Claire it all got a bit ugly, I was probably blowing it out of proportion, but I love her so much and the thought of a past lover in her life wasn't easy for me to handle."

"Did you tell her this?"

"no, I'm not the most articulate guy and I don't find it easy explaining my emotions to people"

"you seem fine to me"

"that's because I don't class you as people"

"thanks"

"You know what I mean." The pair arrived at the crime scene of the third victim. The body was found at the entrance to an old ore mining site just outside of the city's perimeter. The detectives walked roughly thirty yards from where they parked their squad car to see a pile of small to medium sized rocks stacked on top of the victim's body. The head had been revealed by what looked like animals rummaging around to find what was underneath, the face had been pecked at, parts of the skull had been revealed. The hot summer sun beaming down onto the dusty surface didn't help with the aroma that was emanating from the now rotting corpse. Steven looked back towards the city and noticed just how quiet it was out here "who called it in?"

"A dog walker happened upon it yesterday around mid-morning, Detective Smith interviewed him, but he didn't have too much information. He was just in the wrong place at the right time" Geoffrey responded.

"What can you tell me about the Victim?"

"Mr Mark Jones, operations manager at Carson's distribution, a factory on the east side of the city."

"Next to the Shinewater shopping centre?"

"that's the one, he's five feet eleven inches, blonde hair, brown eyes, thirty-five years of age, no children or spouse."

"How was he killed?",

"like our last victim, asphyxiation but again he wasn't killed here, tracks suggest he was transported here by a small vehicle, possibly in the boot, then dumped here to be found two days later by a passer-by buried under a pile of rocks to be hidden from view"

"Doesn't that seem strange to you?"

"what part?" snorted Geoffrey

"why awkwardly bury someone under a pile of rock when it is just as easy to dig a shallow grave in this soft earth. And why bring the body here, there's plenty of places to dump a body on the outskirts of Hightower, what's so special about this site."

"I'll look into it when we get back to the precinct, but first we should head to his work."

"Agreed" Steven and Geoffrey walked back to the police car positioned at the base of the mining site where the body was found. They travelled to the east part of the city passing the site of the first victim and the precinct on the way. "What's the plan for when you get home tonight" Geoffrey asked

"I'm going to go in and apologise to Claire, I think everything got the better of me and I said some things I didn't mean."

"Seems the right thing from my perspective, Claire is a wonderful woman and you are lucky to have her, I'm sure it's just aggravated you more because of everything that's happening at work."

"Your probably right." The pair arrived at the factory that Mr Jones worked at, it was situated on a trading estate next to the Shinewater shopping centre just as Steven had pointed out earlier. They walked towards the large entrance, which was designed to receive lorries, and caught the attention of the first on-site employee they saw "can we speak to the foreman?" asked Steven as he raised his badge. "Of course," the man dressed in high visible clothing walked towards the office located at the side of the building and leant in towards the PA system. "Matt to the security office, Matt to the security office" echoed across the factory, a few moments past and a short, clean faced gentleman wearing a yellow and orange luminescent jacket and a matching helmet approached the detectives. "I'm detective

Cooper and this is detective Osbourne, are you the foreman?" Steven asked.

"Yes, I'm Matt, what's all this about?"

"we'd like to ask you a few questions about Mr Mark Jones."

"Is he ok? I haven't seen him a few days, he hasn't been returning my calls and when I went round his house no one was home."

"I'm sorry to say Mr Jones was found dead at the old mining site on the outskirts of town".

"Jesus" responded the foreman as he put his hand over his mouth and scratched his beard

"can you think of anyone who would want to hurt Mark?"

"No, not at all Mark wouldn't hurt a fly. I knew he had struggled holding down a job before coming here, so I don't know if that means anything."

"Why did he struggle to hold down previous jobs?"

"I heard from some of the other guys he had a drinking problem, he let it get the better of him and left his former employers no choice."

"How long has he worked here?"

"ummm nearly two years now"

"so why the sudden change in character?"

"I'm not sure but it seems to correlate with when he started dating a girl, he met at a speed dating event. He seemed to think the world of her, women can make you do the craziest things detective."

"I know" Steven responded "do you know how we can contact this girl"

"she works at Shaw's bar on the corner of west street."

"I know the one" Geoffrey added

"do you know her name?"

"no, but I have seen her she's red haired, slim and around five feet six, if that helps"

"it does, thank you for your time"

Steven finished the conversation and walked out of the factory forecourt with Geoffrey and headed to the car. "Might be worth heading to the precinct first, I don't think the bar is open until noon and its ten o'clock" Geoffrey informed Steven as they entered the car. They drove to the precinct, stopping of to collect coffees on the way, once they arrived at the station Steven devised a plan of action. "If you look up the significance of the crime scene, I'll speak to detective Smith and see if we missed anything". Geoffrey walked to his cluttered desk, entered his computer password and began to research the mining site. Steven spotted detective Smith sitting in the break room, sipping tea, he walked in and sat in one of the armchairs positioned opposite. "Hey Smithy, can I pick your brain about the Mr Jones case?"

"I told your partner everything"

"I know I just wanted to double check the information."

"Always so thorough Steven, no wonder cap speaks so highly of you. Anyway, the murder was reported around ten A.M yesterday morning by a dog walker, the body was placed under a pile of rocks, which I thought was weird, forensics said it been there for a couple days, hence the smell. Not really sure what more there is to tell you I didn't have the case long before cap transferred it to you."

"What can you tell me about the dog walker?"

"he was walking a golden retriever, he said he walked his dog up by the mining site every Thursday for a change of scenery"

"was there anything odd about him anything at all?"

"I could smell alcohol on his breath, which was odd considering it was the morning, but he seemed to handle himself well."

"Did you get a name?"

"yeah" detective Smith removed his notebook from the inside pocket of his jacket and flipped through the pages. "Mr Dennehy, ring any bells?"

"not yet" Steven responded as he walked out of the break room and made a beeline for Geoffrey's desk, "anything" he asked detective Osbourne as he whipped a chair from his own desk and sat next to his partner. "not much, the site was closed two years ago due an employee being crushed by a sudden avalanche of rocks."

"Much like how our victim was found"

"exactly, the site was used for mining ore from rocks like limestone, coal and various metals. The site was known for Its rocks, which had a high concentration of silicon. But that is not surprising, did you know on a weight basis, the abundance of silicon in the earth's crust is exceeded only by Oxygen."

"Time to get off Wikipedia Geoffrey."

"you're right" Geoffrey said as he closed the tabs he had been using for research "did Smithy give you anything more?"

"Maybe, the name of the dog walker was Mr Dennehy"

"why does that name ring a bell?"

"I think I know, where's the logbook of AA members?"

Geoffrey rummaged around his desk for a few moments before pulling the photocopied logbook from his top desk drawer, he slapped it on the desktop and pointed his finger at the top row of names. "Well, what do you know" above his finger was the name 'Mr Dennehy', "so this case does link to the others" Geoffrey added.

"Detective Smith also said that Mr Dennehy always walked his dog by the mining site on Thursday mornings, I bet that if our suspect attended these meetings, he would have known that too."

"what's the next step?"

"I'm going to Shaw's bar to interview Mr Jones' girlfriend, I need you to contact the other names on that list. If he is targeting people at these AA meetings, then our next victim may be on that list."

Chapter Twelve:

Apology

Steven grabbed his coat from the back of his office chair, whipped the keys for the squad car off Geoffrey's desk and placed them in his pocket. He briskly walked down the stairs of the precinct and jumped into the vehicle and began his journey towards Shaw's bar. The bar was located on the east side of the city not too far from where the third victim (Mr Jones) worked, Steven parked the car in the car park round the back of the establishment. He walked round to the front building and entered, the bar was dimly lit, a contrast to the bright sunshine he had just been driving in. The walls of the bar were filled with pictures, ornaments and various other Knick knacks, Steven walked to the side of the bar and caught the eye of the barmaid through the gap in the lager pumps. She walked across the bar and leant on the middle of the three pump handles "what can I get for you?" she asked seductively. Steven took his badge from his waist and placed it onto the wooden bar top "I'm looking for a waitress that works here red haired around yay high" he gestured with his hand.

The waitress clocked the badge and started acting more professional,

"that sounds like Laura, I'll get her for you". she lifted the bar hatch and walked out onto the main floor of the bar, she headed over to a table with three employees sitting and eating. She turned and pointed back towards Steven whilst speaking to a girl that matched his description. The girl rose from her seat and ventured over to Steven "you wanted to speak to me?" she said sheepishly.

"Yes, do you know a Mr Mark Jones?"

"yeah, he's my boyfriend"

"when was the last time you saw Mr Jones?"

"Saturday, is he ok?"

"Please take a seat" Steven gestured to a bar stall behind the waitress, she slid it in front of her and propped herself upon it. "I'm sorry to tell you this but Mr Jones was found dead yesterday morning, I'm sorry for your loss". Laura burst into tears, covering her face with her hands, Steven reached for some napkins on the table next to him and handed them to her. She took them from him and began dabbing the tears from her cheeks and blowing her nose. "Is it ok if I ask you a few more questions?" Steven asked sympathetically, she sniffed and sniffled before answering "yes".

"Can you think of anyone who would want to hurt Mr Jones?"

"no, he was a nice guy, he did like a drink and got into arguments sometimes when we went out for dinner together, but he was getting better, we were supposed to be going away this weekend, but I guess that won't be happening now".

"You mentioned the last time you saw him was Saturday, if you two were in a relationship, why didn't you see each other more often?".

"My job is mostly working nights and he worked early hours, that work pattern meant there wasn't much time in the week to see each other."

"You mentioned that he liked a drink, but he was getting better, was he seeing any professional help maybe attending AA meetings?".

"If he was, he didn't tell me about it"

"just a few more questions, I can see you're in distress and I don't want to keep you too long." Before Steven could ask another question the sound of a hand dryer blowing in the men's toilets distracted him, he looked up to see a man in a dark cap, pulled down covering his face, and a long black coat. It couldn't be he thought to himself, he rudely left the waitress he was interviewing and rushed in the direction of the man. He ran round the bar and collided with a waitress carrying a tray of drinks, the assortment of alcoholic cocktails soaked the pairs clothing. Steven had not seen her coming as the pillar of the bar had blocked her from view. He brushed her to the side yelling "sorry" as he chased the man out of the back exit of the bar. He caught up to him just outside of the building and grabbed him by the shoulder, spun him round and stared him in the eyes. "can I help you?" the man asked Steven. Detective Cooper instantly realised that he was not the man he thought he was.

"Sorry, I thought you were someone else" responded Steven as he straightened the man's jacket and headed back inside the bar. He walked back to Laura, grabbed his badge from the bar top "thank you for your time miss, if anything comes up please call me, and take care of yourself". Steven handed a card to the waitress and departed the building, he walked back to his parked vehicle and slumped in, the smell of alcohol coming from his sodden clothes was filling the car. He wound down the passenger side and driver side windows and headed back to the precinct, hopefully Geoffrey had found better information, he thought to himself.

He arrived back at the station; his clothes had started to harden from the various liquids that had soaked into them. As he entered the building and walked up the stairs, he received scowls from other employees, because of the stench of alcohol no doubt. He reached Geoffrey's desk "enjoy yourself at Shaw's bar, did we?" asked Geoffrey referring to the alcohol stains on Stevens shirt.

"I ran into a waitress carrying a tray of drinks whilst chasing a perp" Steven responds as he rung the last drops of alcohol from his white shirt.

"Did you catch him?"

"yeah but he wasn't our guy... please tell me you found something".

"Maybe, of all the names on the list other than Miss Willow, Mr Johnson and Mr Dennehy. Only Miss James is a real person, also excluding Mr Mendeleev who died in 1907 and was responsible for creating the periodic table".

"Been back on Wikipedia have we Geoffrey?"

"anyway, there's a Miss James who lives at fifty-six Wilmington avenue".

"That's one road away from the rec centre that the AA meetings are held"

"that's the one, my guess is it's the same person",

"let's head over there." Steven hurried to leave the precinct as Geoffrey caught up with him outside the building's large blue door. "Stop" cried Geoffrey "I'll head over and drop you back home on the way"

"what why?" asked a confused Steven.

"why, firstly it is four o'clock and you need to be home on time to patch things up with your wife, secondly you smell of alcohol which won't go down too well with Miss James. Also you need to slow down a bit, I know you want to catch this guy, but so do I, you've become more erratic then I've ever seen you, I think you need to take a step back". Steven stared blankly at Geoffrey for a second before responding, "you're right, I've become obsessed with catching this person I've let it get in the way of my relationship not to mention my health".

"It's ok Steven, I'll drop you home and continue the case, I've got your back, not for the first time" Geoffrey winked.

"Ok Geoffrey, and thanks, thanks for everything".

They entered the vehicle and headed to Stevens home; Geoffrey pulled the vehicle up outside.

"I'm actually quite nervous" said Steven as he aired out his shirt by shaking the collar to cool himself down.

"You'll be fine" added Geoffrey "just tell her what you told me this morning, now get out I've got a job to do". Steven opened the car door and left the vehicle, before closing the door he said "thanks again Geoffrey, I'll see you tomorrow" Geoffrey nodded and drove off after Steven had swung the door closed. He began slowly walking the path of his home before reaching the door, he stopped and took a huge deep breath. He opened the door and walked towards the sideboard and placed his effects upon it before hanging his coat on the coat rack beside it. He walked into the living and saw Lily sitting and playing with her Miss Millicent doll "hey sweetie".

"Hi dad" she replied

He turned to see his wife sitting at the table in the kitchen, she looked up and placed the pen she was holding onto the pad in front of her. He gulped and walked towards her, stepping from the carpet of the living onto the cold hard marble floor of the kitchen. "Hi" he sighed

"hi"

"I'm not good at these things so I'm just going to come out and say it. I am sorry, I should never have told you what you can and cannot do, I reacted the way I did because I am afraid of losing you both. I have been stressed out with work and when you told me about Alex it just got too much for me, I am sorry".

"Why do you think you're going to lose us?"

"I don't know when you told me your ex-husband had been round, I got jealous, don't ask me why. When I found out you kept a secret, I thought you were hiding something from me, but maybe you just didn't know how to tell me".

"You can be a real idiot sometimes; you know that don't you?"

"yeah, but I am your idiot".

Claire stood up from her chair and walked over to her husband, she threw her arms around him and said "yes, you are my idiot, and why do you smell of alcohol?".

Chapter Thirteen: Epiphany

The Cooper family enjoyed their evening, eating dinner, watching tv and playing with Lily and her toys. They decided to go to bed early as the next day was going to be a big one.

Steven and Claire were woken by Lily jumping up and down on their bed, holding her Miss Millicent doll. "Today's my party" she repeated in a high pitch voice, Steven rubbed his eyes "what time is it" he asked Claire. "Nine" Claire responded whist stretching out her arms "we need to get up and start setting up the house for Lily's party". Lily screamed with excitement and leapt from the bed before sprinting out of the bedroom. Steven rolled out of bed and walked into the on-suite bathroom whilst Claire headed downstairs to make a few cups of coffee. Steven got himself dressed and made his way downstairs and was greeted by a hot cup of Columbian coffee sitting on the coffee table.

Claire was emptying party games, banners and hats from bags and placing the contents on the dining room table. Steven grabbed the large pink banner, with happy birthday printed in large bubble writing in the middle. He dragged a chair from the dining table into the living room, propped himself up on it and began hanging the banner. He stepped back and checked to see if it was level, which Claire told him it was not, he corrected the banner and began decorating the rest of the house. Once they were finished the inside of the home looked like an arts and crafts store, the living room was clad with banners and streamers, pin the tail on the donkey was set up in the middle and a table to the side destined to be filled with gift from all their guests. The dining room table was filled with various party food and colourful plates and napkins. Claire ran upstairs and got herself ready for the party, she returned wearing a colourful, flowery dress decorated with red, yellow and orange petals. "You look beautiful" Steven said as he caught sight of her, he placed his arms around her and began the sway to the music he had put on the stereo system whilst she was getting ready. The moment was interrupted by the doorbell ringing, "that'll be the first guest" Claire said as she broke Stevens grip and walked towards the front door. Over the next hour or so Guests arrived, from family members, to neighbours to colleagues of Claire. The house held around fifteen adults, although they were outnumbered by screaming children. "Time for pin the tail on the donkey" Claire called to the kids playing in the garden. They all let out a large scream before cramping themselves in the living room to watch the game unfold, the doorbell rang, as Steven was closest, he decided to answer it. He opened the door to reveal his partner Geoffrey dressed in blue jeans and a charcoal shirt, holding a small gift which was poorly wrapped in sparkly red wrapping paper.

"Just in time for pin the tail on the donkey" Steven said as he stepped aside to let Geoffrey enter his home.

"Oh, good my favourite game" he walked into the living room and placed the present on the corresponding table. Lily saw Geoffrey and ran towards him to give him a big hug "Uncle Geoff" she yelled as she buried her cheek into his stomach

"happy birthday Lily" he responded slightly winded.

"Hi Geoffrey" Claire added "come on Lily your up first." Lily let go of Geoffrey and ran into the centre of the room to start the game. Geoffrey walked past Steven, headed into the kitchen, opened the fridge, pulled out a beer and re-joined Steven in the living room. "Help yourself" Steven quipped

"don't mind if I do" Geoffrey answered whilst dribbling the lager down his chin and mopping it up with his hand.

"What happened with Miss James yesterday?"

"can't switch off can you, it was a bust, she never visited the rec centre, didn't know any of the other victims, I think this time it was just a coincidence, anyway enjoy your daughters party, let the weekend squad work the case, god I sound like you".

"That's a shame, hopefully the weekend squad will find something that we've missed"

"hopefully, something just seems strange, if this guy is targeting you why is the only thing connecting you two the letter that was found on the third victim".

"Well, that's not entirely true"

"what do you mean?".

"The day the body of Mr Johnson was called in, I arrived home and found a note taped to my front door"

"and your telling me this now!" Geoffrey yelled.

"Keep your voice down, Claire doesn't know about this"

"what did the letter say?"

"it said, recognise me yet?" Steven whispered

"that implies you've seen him multiple times, have you?"

"yeah I've seen him three maybe four times".

"What the hell Steven! You may have seen our suspect multiple times and you didn't tell me, he's left you messages at your home and you didn't tell me, what else are you not telling me?". Claire overheard the conversation; she moved her focus from this children's game and towards Steven.

"What's this about murderers appearing at our home?" She pressed; the room was filled with a deafening silence as she stopped the music.

"It's nothing, honestly"

"It doesn't sound like nothing; it sounds like dangerous people are setting foot on our property and you've got the audacity to keep it a secret from me!" The guest remained silent, awkwardly stood in between the argument.

"That's rich coming from you"

"what's that supposed to mean?"

"your ex-husband suddenly appears back in your life and you keep it a secret from me and Lily!".

"Out" Claire cried as she pointed to the front door as her eyes became watery. "Get out of this house now!" Steven paused for a moment before marching upstairs to his bedroom, he grabbed handfuls of socks, boxers, shirts, and trousers from his chest of drawers and wardrobe. He stuffed them into a small suitcase he retrieved from the corner of the room, he just managed to zip it up before storming back downstairs and slamming the door as he exited his family home.

Geoffrey was waiting outside "come stay with me for a bit, just until all this blows over"

"thanks Geoffrey"

The pair entered Geoffrey's red town car and headed over to Geoffrey's home. "Look, if we're going to find this killer we need to work together, I can't have you keeping facts about the case hidden from me" said Geoffrey.

"I know I can't, but at the time I wasn't sure if the letter pertained to the case or not"

"why wouldn't you think it related to the case?".

"When I received it, the two cases were fairly fresh, I wasn't sure if they linked and I thought keeping the letter a secret was the right idea, I see now that it wasn't".

The pair arrived at a small apartment block; Geoffrey drove the car round to the allocated parking site behind the building. The detectives exited the vehicle and began scaling the metal staircase, which was located on the side of the building. The staircase lead round to the front of the building where Geoffrey's apartment was located on the first floor. He pulled his keys from his pocket, slid the key in the keyhole and opened the door. "It's not much, but it' home" he said as he encouraged Steven inside. Steven was greeted by a musky smell, the living room was untidy, sofa cushions on the floor, empty bottles on the coffee table and stains on the carpet. "It's like the Ritz" Steven said sarcastically

"and this is where you'll be sleeping", Geoffrey walked over to the unorganised sofa, propped the back cushions up and retrieved the smaller throw cushions from the floor. Steven dumped his suitcase at the side of the sofa and slumped onto it. The room fell silent for a few moments before Geoffrey spoke "I'm starving, want to order some food?". He shuffled together a collection of takeaway menus that were scattered on the small wooded coffee table situated in front of the sofa. "Pick one" he said whilst handing the menus to Steven. Steven took the collection of leaflets from Geoffrey shuffled through them and finally settled on a curry house a few roads away. He handed the chosen menu to Geoffrey "ah, good choice, what would you like?"

"I'll have whatever you have?"

"vindaloo it is then". Geoffrey took the menu from Steven and headed into the kitchen to place the order. Steven fell back into his seat, how could his life fall apart so quickly, who would want this for him, how was he going to win Claire back. All these thoughts flew around his brain as he could hear Geoffrey trying to get a free naan bread with the order. He re-entered the room, Steven with his eyes closed did not see him return, "what shall we do?" asked

Geoffrey "you can't just sit there moping all evening".

"At the moment Geoffrey, I think I need to do the only thing I know how to do, work, if I can solve this case I can get Claire back and everything will go back to normal".

"Right, that doesn't seem healthy, but I have to admit I want this case out the way".

Geoffrey cleared the coffee table of stacked dirty plates and used coffee mugs, he took them to the kitchen and dumped them by the sink. He returned with a cloth to wipe the table clean "that'll be our workstation" said a pleased Geoffrey, Steven was not as equally impressed, but he would work with what he had. The pair scrawled down facts about the three cases on pieces of scrap Geoffrey had taken from the drawers to the unit holding up the fingerprint smeared television, adjacent from the sofa. They kept the three case facts separate except for what linked them, those facts were placed in the middle of the table. "so far, the links we have are all three victims had a drink problem but were trying to get a hold of their addiction, either the victim, or someone involved, attended the same AA meetings. That suggests that our killer attended the same meetings, that's how they selected their victims" explained Steven.

"We need to look at this in a different way"

"what do you suggest?"

"well, the killer is clearly singling you out here, they even referred to you by name. We need to compile information about the person you've seen, what can you tell me about them?".

"I've never really got a clear view of them, from what I can make out they're around six feet tall, the same height as me, short dark hair, but I only saw them from behind".

"when was that?"

"at the awards night, he was selling raffle tickets to Claire and I saw him from across the room".

"You saw him that long ago" said a shocked Geoffrey "well that means Claire got a good look at him?".

"No, when I asked her, she couldn't remember much, she'd had a couple drinks by this point. I saw him in the park the next day, but it was a bright day, he was all the way across the field and when I asked Claire if she recognised him, he had gone".

"Ok, when else did you see him?" asked Geoffrey whilst writing down what Steven was saying

"then I received the first note, stuck to my front door. The next time I saw him was when I was leaving the geology store and I chased him through the alleyways. He was wearing the same coat and hat he was wearing at the park, that's why I was sure it was him, but as you know I lost him, and the security footage turned up nothing".

"And that's all the times you've see him?"

"I thought I saw him in Shaw's bar, but it turned out to be someone else, I ruined a perfectly good shirt that day".

"Yeah the smell of alcohol is still in my car, so all we've got is he's six feet tall and has short dark hair, sometimes wears a long black coat and a dark hat".

"Can you think of anyone who would want this situation for you?"

"I looked though old cases, I had a few ideas but most of them are either still in prison or don't live in or around the city".

"What about someone you haven't put away? Someone in your personal life?"

"like whom?" Steven questioned

"Alex? Claire's ex-husband"

"yeah, good one Geoffrey".

"I'm serious" Steven rolled his eyes "think about it, he hasn't been around for years and suddenly he re-appears just as these murders start popping up. You told me he had a drink problem, just like our victims and not to mention he could be targeting you because you married Claire and treat his daughter like your own".

Steven slumped back in his chair; eyes wide whilst scratching his chin "you might just be onto something Geoffrey" said Steven as he sat back up in his chair. "But if it is him, Claire would've recognised him at the awards night?"

"you said it yourself, she'd had a couple of drinks and she hadn't seen him in years, she wasn't exactly looking for her ex-husband".

Steven came to a sudden realisation, maybe Geoffrey was right, could Alex be the murderer, if they were to find out they would have to investigate him. His thought process was cut short by the piercing sound of the doorbell being rung "that's the food". Geoffrey leapt from his seat greeted the delivery driver and took the packaged food from him, not before tipping him, and closing the door. He rummaged through the bag and looked back up at Steven with a frown "they didn't put in the extra naan."

Chapter Fourteen:
Keep your enemies close

They enjoyed their spicy curry, Geoffrey more so than Steven, they collected up the scrap paper with all the information they had written down and stacked it in a pile. Geoffrey went to his bedroom and returned with an uncovered single duvet "I've not got any spare pillows; you'll have to use the sofa cushions".

"This really is the Ritz" Steven responded, he took the duvet from Geoffrey and threw it over himself.

"sleep tight" said Geoffrey sarcastically as he walked back towards his bedroom. Steven tucked his knees up to fit on the small sofa, he knew he was not going to get to sleep. There was too much wracking around his brain, not to mention how uncomfortable the sofa was. He laid awake all-night tossing and turning, trying to find a comfortable position. Eventually the sunlight, peering through the blinds by the front door, told him it was morning. He sat up moving his head from side to side, clicking his neck in the process. He left the sofa and walked to the kitchen to make himself a coffee, he rummaged through the kitchen drawers to find a spoon to stir his piping hot coffee. He turned round to see Geoffrey standing behind him wearing nothing but a pair of white Y fronts. "Open those drawers a little louder, I couldn't quite hear it" Geoffrey said sarcastically as he rubbed the sleep from his eyes.

"Sorry, can I at least make you a coffee?"

"go on then"

Steven made the pair a coffee each and returned to the living room and sat on the duvet which was scrunched on the sofa. "So, what's the plan today" Geoffrey asked as he sipped his hot coffee, burning his tongue in the process.

"I think we need to look into Alex, where he's staying, what his job is and his whereabouts during the murders".

"We should let the weekend squad know were working the case"

"it might be best to keep it between us, just until we have a bit more information".

"Keeping secrets didn't work out too well for you last time did it?"

"we will only keep it a secret until we know more".

"Fine" said Geoffrey reluctantly, "go take a shower, you stink, there's a spare blue towel on the rack beside the shower".

Steven finished up his coffee and headed for the bathroom, to prepare himself for the day. They both dressed casually for the day, steven wearing dark jeans and a white polo shirt and Geoffrey wearing the same jeans from yesterday and a grey t-shirt. They left Geoffrey's apartment, got in his pedestrian car and headed for the precinct. "What's Alex's surname" asked Geoffrey

"Dawson, when I married Claire, she decided to change Lily's surname to Cooper, along with her own".

"When we get to work, I'll head in and search him in the database, it'll be best if you wait in the car, that way we won't attract too much attention". Steven nodded in agreement, they arrived at the precinct and executed the plan as discussed. Steven waited in the car as the warm morning sun was slowly turning it into an oven. Luckily, Geoffrey did not take too long, he skipped out of the precinct entrance and hoped back into the driver's seat. "thirty-six Fulton avenue" Informed Geoffrey as he locked his seatbelt in place and started the engine.

"If it does turn out to be Alex, how will you tell Claire or Lily? Will you even tell them?" asked Geoffrey.

"we will cross that bridge when we get there", Steven remained deep in thought during the car journey only responding to Geoffrey with accepting hums. They arrived at the address of Claire's ex-husband, "park a few houses away, we don't want to be seen". The two detectives sat in the now boiling vehicle and waited until they saw movement at the home they were stalking. Around an hour had passed and a blue vehicle pulled up outside, out stepped a tall dark-haired man, "that matches your description?".

"Yeah, but I can't say for certain if it's him or not"

The man locked his car, walked towards his home and entered. "What's the next step?"

"we need to speak to him and find out information, but I can't do it".

"Why not?"

"if he is our guy, he'll recognise me straight away, you need to go in and get all the information"

"right, ok, no problem" mumbled Geoffrey

"you'll be fine, just get in, gets his whereabouts during the murders and get out, simple as that".

Geoffrey took a deep breath before exiting the vehicle, the door barely closed behind him as it slipped off his now sweaty palm. Steven watched him walk the pavement and towards the from door. Geoffrey was greeted at the door by a blonde woman before being welcomed in. Steven sat in the car for almost an hour, sweating and periodically checking his phone to see if Claire had tried to contact him, nothing. Geoffrey emerged from the house said what seemed to be a cheerful goodbye and walked back to his car. He had barely got in the car before Steven said "well?"

"I'll tell you when we get back to mine, I'm starving though, want to get some food on the way".

Geoffrey pulled away from the curb and drove back home, stopping at a local sandwich shop on the way. Steven spent the entire journey agitated, tapping his foot in the footwell of the car. They finally reached Geoffrey's place and walked the metal staircase towards his first-floor apartment. They sat on the sofa, Steven placed his wrapped sandwich on the coffee table as Geoffrey began unwrapping and eating his. "well, what did he say?" said an impatient Steven

"he was out of town for work last week, in Capital City, and didn't get back until Saturday night, meaning he can't have killed Mis Willow. His girlfriend, the blonde who answered the door, vouched for him on the murder of Mr Johnson, they were together at home that night. And his whereabouts for the murder of Mr Jones was a little bit hazy, he was on his own at home around the time of the crime, but the fact he was not around for the first two murders suggests he may not be involved in the third".

"Or he's working with someone else"

"maybe, but that's a bit of a stretch Steven".

"at the moment he's our only lead, he matches the description and he's got a motive"

"even you said you weren't sure if he was the guy you've been seeing, and as far as a motive goes it's a circumstantial".

"Whose side are you on?" asked Steven aggressively

"yours Steven, but I don't want to put an innocent man in prison!". The argument between the pair was cut short by Stevens phone ringing, he pulled it from his pocket and look at the screen. He looked up at Geoffrey "it's Claire", he got up from the sofa and walked to the kitchen for some privacy. He answered the phone "hi Claire"

"what's this about Geoffrey interrogating Alex?"

"how do you know about that?"

"Alex just called me and told me your partner visited him at his home, you need to let this go Steven, I'm not seeing him, he just wants to see his daughter".

"That's not why we were there, we had reason to believe he was involved in these murders"

"that's ridiculous, I know he wasn't the nicest of guys when we were together, but domestic abuse is a far stretch from serial killer" "we are just exploring every avenue; did you call to just to tell me off?".

"No, I spoke to Christina from work and she reminded me of this parents intro day at Lily's new school".

"Ok, I'll be there, when is it?"

"that's the problem its Wednesday evening, that's the same night we have tickets to the opening of 'Genesis garden'."

"Well, you find someone to go with you to the gardens, I'll attend the intro day"

"are you sure?".

"of course, I know how much you like that stuff, just enjoy yourself"

"thanks Steven"

"one more thing before you go?" Steven just caught Claire before she hung up. "What about Tuesday night?"

"what about it"

"it's date night, we haven't missed one in five years".

"Things are tough at the moment, I need to put Lily first, I still love you Steven, I just think we need a bit of space".

"I will be there regardless if you come or not"

"ok, I will see" Claire hung up the phone and Steven placed it back in his pocket before heading into the living room with Geoffrey.

"What did Claire say?"

"apparently, Alex recognised you and asked Claire why we were investigating him".

"Ah right, what did you tell her?"

"I told her the truth"

"and"

"I don't think she was very happy with it, but it is what it is".

"Perhaps we should put this on hold for the rest of the evening, let's just relax I can find one of those old films you like and we can just try to forget about all this, for now at least."

"I think taking a break is a good idea". The two detectives spent the evening enjoying each other's company, they ordered pizzas watched movies and for a moment Steven forget all the problems in his personal and professional life. They went to bed early to get a head start on the next day.

Chapter Fifteen:
No more secrets

Steven slept better than the night before, he still did not sleep well, he followed the same routine as the morning before. He went to the kitchen to make himself a coffee, this time being quiet as to not wake up Geoffrey. He went for a shower after he had finished his coffee, he spent his time waiting for Geoffrey to wake by cleaning his living room, he threw away all takeaway containers, moved dirty crockery into the kitchen and organised the paperwork the pair had worked on. Finally, Geoffrey woke up and walked into the living room, thankfully wearing more than he was the morning before thought Steven. "come on get ready" Steven said whilst checking his watch

"ok mum, this I why I don't have a roommate, or a girlfriend for that matter". Geoffrey got himself ready for work whilst Steven finished cleaning the front room. Once they collected their stuff, they left Geoffrey's apartment, headed down the outside steps and entered the squad car parked next to Geoffrey's pedestrian car. "I need you to look into Alex's alibi's, call his work and confirm he was out of town" asked Steven as Geoffrey pulled away from his apartment building.

"And what are you going to do?"

"I'm going to speak to the Captain, give him a rundown of the cases, apparently he's getting grief from the commissioner about these murders. If I keep him informed hopefully, he won't consider taking the cases away from us and giving them to another detective".

"Why would he do that?"

"he might think I'm too close to this case and bring in someone with a more unbiased view".

"are you too close?" Geoffrey asked, Steven gave Geoffrey a discerning look, Geoffrey gulped.

The two detectives arrived at the precinct, scaled its front steps, walked to the first floor and entered the bullpen. Steven went to his desk, as did Geoffrey, Steven removed his coat and placed it on the back of his chair. He collected the files from his workspace and walked towards the Captains office, he looked over at Geoffrey who was on the phone and gave him a nod. He reached the Captains office and gave the open door a gentle tap to get the Captains attention. Captain Luther was on the phone, but he noticed Steven's presence and gestured him towards a seat, Steven obliged and closed the door behind him. "yes…. Yes, I understand commissioner… ok bye" said Captain Luther as he slammed the phone on the receiver. He leant forward, brought his elbows up onto the desk and rested his chin on his hands "please tell me you've got something good".

"maybe, I believe we've found the link, all the victims are alcoholics that attended the same AA meetings, except the third victim, however his body was discovered someone who did attend the meetings".

"Good, that would suggest that the murderer would've attended the same meetings, that's how they selected their victims".

"Exactly, although they do not have an accurate record of attendants, it is alcoholic anonymous after all, we do however have a suspect, Geoffrey is following up on his alibis now. He matches the vague description of the person we saw on the security footage". And other sightings he thought to himself, "he is also a recovering alcoholic himself, although there's no evidence to suggest he attended the meetings".

"How do you know he's a recovering alcoholic?"

"his name is Alex Dawson, he's my wife's ex-husband".

"What the hell Steven, you are too close to this case, the killer personally targeting you and now your number one suspect is your wife's ex-husband. You are one of my best detectives I don't want to have to remove you from the case, but I don't feel like I'm being left much of an option, therefore I'm putting myself on this case with you". The Captains speech was interrupted by Geoffrey bursting into the office "detective Osbourne, please knock before entering!".

"Sorry Raymond but it's important, I have just got off the phone with Alex's work, he was out of town the week of Miss Willows murder. But he left early Thursday morning, claiming he was sick, that would have given him more than enough time to get back from Capital City for the murder of Miss Willow".

Captain Luther rose from his seat "so your number one suspect fed you a false alibi and could be anywhere right now? Geoffrey prep the interrogation room and don't call me Raymond, Steven you and I are going to bring this guy in". He swiped the jacket from the coat rack behind him, threw it over his shoulders and marched out of the precinct, with Steven scrambling behind. They entered the Captain's black, undercover police car, switched on the blue and red lights along with the siren. "Where does he live?" asked Captain Luther

"Thirty-Six Fulton Avenue" replied Steven still trying to regain his breath. The pair sped over to Alex's house in a flash, Steven spent the journey holding onto the handle at the side of the car, due to the speed at which the Captain was driving. Once they arrived, the Captain leapt from his seat and out of the car, he ran to the front door of the suspects house and banged hard three times. The door swung open "are you Alex Dawson?" barked Captain Luther "umm yes", Captain Luther grabbed the suspect, flipped him round and cuffed his hands behind his back, Alex's face was now pressed against the frame of the door to his home. "Alex Dawson I'm placing you under arrest on suspicion of the murder of Miss Willow, Mr Johnson and Mr Jones".

"what that's ridiculous!" cried Alex as he was pulled away by the police Captain "I gave my alibis to detective Osbourne; it couldn't have been me!".

"Save it" yelled Captain Luther as he walked Alex down the path of his home and tucked his head under the roof to the car and into the backseat. Steven watched the entire process in silence, he could not help but think about Claire and Lily and how this news might affect them, he entered the passenger's seat of the undercover car and buckled his seat beat. Steven spent the slower return journey staring out the window, deep in thought.

Once they returned to the precinct, Captain Luther retrieved the suspect from the back of the car, walked him into the station and handed him to a waiting Geoffrey "take him to the interrogation room" ordered Captain Luther, Geoffrey followed his orders and Captain Luther marched back to his office, slowly joined by Steven. "I think its best if I interrogate him" said Captain Luther

"with all due respect Captain, this is my case".

"With all due respect detective Cooper, that is your wife's ex-husband in there, if he is the killer, he was targeting you, I think your judgment may be blurred".

"But Captain"

"no Steven!" Captain Luther interrupted "I'm interrogating him, and that decision is final, leave the cases on my desk and you can watch from the adjoining room". Steven stormed out of the office and outside the building, Geoffrey, now sitting back at his desk, spotted him and chose to follow him. Steven was joined by Geoffrey by the steps of the precinct "has he taken you off the case?" asked Geoffrey.

"No not yet, but I feel it's only a matter of time, he's conducting the interrogation of Mr Dawson".

"Maybe that's a good thing, he can take a more objective approach"

"yeah, maybe".

"What's more important you solve the case, or the case being solved?".

"When did you become to mature one?"

"I've had a great partner to learn from". Steven smirked at Geoffrey and Geoffrey returned with a wink "come on let us go and watch the interrogation". The two detectives re-entered the building and entered the room adjoining the interrogation room. Steven stood with his arms folded, staring at his wife's ex-husband through the two-way glass, Captain Luther was sat with his back to the two detectives. "I already told detective Osbourne that I was away with work, I couldn't have murdered Miss Willow" pleaded Mr Dawson.

"Well, detective Osbourne followed up on that alibi and your work said you headed home early because you were sick, Giving you more than enough time to commit the crime, so how do you explain that?".

Alex let out a huge sigh "I was away with work that week, but I left early to meet up with someone...".

"Who?" asked an impatient Captain Luther

"a woman"

"you were cheating on your girlfriend?".

"Yes, but I couldn't tell the truth to detective Osbourne because my girlfriend was within ear shot and she obviously doesn't know".

"Have you got any evidence to suggest you are telling the truth?"

"we met at a motel, just off junction six five or so miles from the city. I don't have a receipt, but I was certainly there".

"You've lied to us before why should I believe you this time?" Captain Luther asked rhetorically "I'm going to detain you for seventy-two hours, just until we can clear all this up".

"But"

"I don't want to hear another word out of you" Captain Luther left his seat and exited the interrogation room. He immediately joined detective Cooper and detective Osbourne in the adjoining room. "Osbourne, I need you to check out that alibi, Steven I need you to go to Mr Dawson's home and speak to his girlfriend, see if she can give us any more information". Geoffrey gave a nod of acceptance and left the room, "wait" called Captain Luther stopping Steven from leaving. "You don't look too good detective, you look tired, your facial hair is untidy, and your clothes are scruffy, is everything ok?".

"Claire and I had a little disagreement, I'm currently staying at Geoffrey's', but I'm sure everything will be back to normal soon".

"ok, but if you need anything, whether it is about the case or not, you know where my door is"

"thanks Captain, I appreciate it".

Chapter Sixteen: The Last Note

Steven gathered his effects from his desk, made his way out of the police station and entered the squad car that he and Geoffrey shared. He was both annoyed and relieved that Captain Luther had put himself on the case. Annoyed that he had let the case get the better of him, which Captain Luther saw. And relieved that the Captain had not taken the case from him. Steven arrived at thirty-six Fulton avenue, the home of Alex Dawson and his girlfriend. He parked the vehicle outside and began to walk up the path towards the front door, he knocked a few times. The door was opened by an average height, blonde woman with tears running down her face. "You arrested Alex, why?" she cried

"I understand this is a hard time for you miss, but would you be able to answer a few questions. It could help clear Alex's name and return him home sooner". She wiped the tears from her eyes and gave a quick snivel before saying "ok, come in". Steven entered the modest, suburban house and took a seat on the wooded chairs at the end on the dining room table. "My names Brenda" said Alex's girlfriend as she took a seat opposite Steven.

"Brenda, how long have you and Alex been together?"

"we've been together for around a year now, but we've known each other for about three".

"And how long have you lived here?"

"six months, we met when we both lived in capital city, Alex still goes back for work sometimes. And we decided to get away from that backwards city and get a home here in Hightower".

"Are you aware of Alex's past, as an alcoholic?"

"yes, he was working on his addiction when I met him and that is one of the main reasons we moved here, almost a fresh start kind of thing".

"Is there anything peculiar you can think of, sneaking out late, saying he's somewhere and being somewhere else anything like that?".

"No, detective what are you insinuating?"

"I'm not implying anything Miss I'm just trying to prove your boyfriend is as innocent as you say he is".

"well, if he has done anything odd, I have not noticed it, anyway he gave your partner all his whereabouts yesterday, didn't he?". Steven thought to mention his false alibi, but Brenda knowing would not help the case.

"Thanks for your time Brenda". Steven rose from his seat and walked towards the exit, "look after yourself miss, if Alex is innocent, he will be back before you know it". Steven gave a small smile and walked back to his car, he slumped in and checked his watch, four o'clock. He drove back to the precinct to see if Geoffrey had confirmed Mr Dawson's second alibi. Once back he entered the building and walked over the Geoffrey's desk "did it check out?" he asked.

"Yeah, the man I contacted remembered him, he also used his real name to sign in, rookie mistake if you are going to cheat". Steven looked quizzically at Geoffrey "anyway, what did his girlfriend say?"

"Brenda didn't have much to say, she's not aware of his womanising, and they have not been together long". Captain Luther joined the two detectives at Geoffrey's desk

"by the looks on your faces neither of you have good news. Go home detectives we will get an early start on this tomorrow, and Geoffrey, maybe you can find time to clean your desk" said Captain Luther as he picked up a coffee stained folder.

"Ok, Ray" Geoffrey hurried to his feet, collected his things and rushed out of the precinct as to not get more grief off the Captain, Steven followed behind with a smirk on his face.

Once in the vehicle and on the road to Geoffrey's apartment Geoffrey asked, "do you honestly think that Alex is our man?"

"I know the evidence doesn't suggest it, but something will pop up that will even prove him innocent or guilty, I can feel it".

"You're always so optimistic Steven"

"yeah, or stupid".

The pair arrived at Geoffrey's apartment, they both slumped onto the sofa and took a deep breath. Geoffrey reached for the remote and switched on the television, "I'm going to call Claire" Steven said as he pulled the phone from his pocket and walked towards the kitchen, Geoffrey did not respond. A few moments passed and Steven returned to the living room "what did she say?" asked Geoffrey

"she didn't answer" replied Steven.

"maybe she needs more time, isn't it date night tomorrow night? You'll see her then, won't you?"

"I hope so, I said I'll be there, but she didn't say otherwise. I'm slowly letting everything slip Geoffrey"

"I'm sure she'll be there, you two are meant to be together".

"Thanks Geoffrey, but I'm not sure it's as simple as that".

The pair spent the evening trying to find evidence that ties Alex to any one of these cases, they scattered the papers they had used a few night ago, onto the coffee table. Hi alibi's checkout, he has no previous charges, other than drunk and disorderly. There was only one avenue Steven could think of

"I think our best angle is motive. If we can pressure him into admitting he is doing this to get his family back, that's our best shot" Explained Steven.

"Do you honestly think he'd go to all this trouble just to sabotage your marriage, and in some way that would win Claire and Lily back?".

"Honestly no, but it's all we've got" Steven organised the paperwork on the table and stacked it to one side, "I'm going to get some sleep, we will devise a plan of action tomorrow" Steven said as he covered his mouth whist yawning. Geoffrey got off the sofa and headed for his bedroom, before closing the door he yelled "good night, sleep tight" Steven smirked.

The next morning Steven awoke at his normal time, from a satisfying slumber, he stretched out his arms and legs and went to make a coffee in the kitchen. He was shocked to see Geoffrey already awake, showered and dressed and preparing them both a drink. "About time you got up" joked Geoffrey

"what's the matter, couldn't sleep?"

"no, I set an early alarm so we could get a head start on this case. After all I am sick of you living here and the sooner we solve the case, the sooner you go home".

"I'm actually in shock"

"at what, the fact you're not a delightful roommate?".

"no, the fact you've got an alarm clock", Geoffrey smirked and threw a towel at Steven.

"go get ready, I'll put this coffee in a flask for you", Steven headed to the bathroom whilst Geoffrey made the pair hot drinks, Steven reappeared, smelling fresh and wearing new clothes, although not dissimilar to what he wore every workday. They left the apartment, entered the squad car and began their journey to the precinct "if we set up a workstation in the briefing room, and add the Mr Jones case to the other two cases, with Captain Luther's help we may find something we've missed" Said Steven hopefully.

"Even with everything going on your still managing to remain positive"

"I spent years being negative, Claire taught me to be more positive and I'm not going to stop now".

The pair arrived at the station and followed out their plan, they placed each case in the centre of a white board and the links between them met in the middle, drinking, AA meetings and Steven. Captain Luther came to join them,

Steven checked his watch "Captain it's ten A.M have you just got in? you're never late?".

"Yeah what gives Ray?" added Geoffrey as the Captain rolled his eyes.

"I think Mr Dawson has proven his innocence" replied Captain Luther

"how's that?" asked Steven

"I've just returned from a new crime scene this morning; this was found there". Captain Luther passed a bagged piece of evidence over the Steven. In the bag was another note that read 'You're running out of time'. "I'm not an expert on being in two places at once, but how our murderer can be sat in a holding cell and be committing crimes at the same time is beyond me" said Captain Luther as he sat back in his chair and folded his arms.

Chapter Seventeen:
The fourth victim

Steven and Geoffrey looked at one another for a moment, Steven turned back to Captain Luther "where is the body?" he asked.

"Detective, it might be better to let someone else step in on this case, it may be getting too much for you to handle".

"Don't take this case away from me!" cried Steven "we're so close to solving it, you need to trust me".

"I don't know Steven" said Captain Luther undecidedly.

"Please Captain, trust me". Captain Luther looked Steven in the eyes and let out an audible sigh "the crime scene is on the corner of thirty-fourth street".

"Thanks Captain." Steven grabbed his coat and Geoffrey did the same, before he left the briefing room Steven was stopped by Captain Luther placing his hand firmly on his chest "don't let me down detective" Captain Luther said

"I won't captain", responded a steely eyed Steven as he and his partner scurried out of the precinct and jumped into the police vehicle. "What do you think the note meant?" Geoffrey questioned as he revved the engine before pulling away.

"I honestly haven't got a clue, but whatever it is it can't be good". The pair arrived at the crime scene; the body was hidden from view by a blue tarp. The corner of the street had a temporary perimeter indicated by the police tape; the roads were still busy with drivers slowing near the scene to gain a better view. The forensic scientist had arrived in the morning with Captain Luther and had already partly investigated the scene. "what have we got?" asked Steven as he and Geoffrey approached the scientist.

"Female, approximately Five feet Six, twenty-two years of age, cause of death asphyxiation, time of death around midnight".

"I've got a question" Geoffrey added "what is that smell, it smells like rotten eggs" he asked whilst closing his nostrils with his thumb and fore finger.

"The smell is coming from the drain next to the victim, that odour is caused by hydrogen sulphide gas, interestingly sulphur is odourless, its only when it reacts with other elements, like hydrogen, that it releases the smell of rotten eggs".

"Right..." responded Geoffrey as he walked under the police tape and encouraged Steven to join him. Steven followed and walked over to the blue tarp covering the body. He pulled the end away to reveal a young, pretty, caramel Blonde woman, her neck was covered in bruises confirming the cause of death. "I find it so much harder to deal with when their so young" Steven said as he looked at Geoffrey. "I think our killer wanted this body found right away, much like Miss Willow and Mr Johnson. But the body of Mr Jones was hidden on the outskirts of town, I think they have planned the order that theses bodies needed to be found".

"But why kill Mr Jones a few days earlier and hide his body away to be found later?".

"When I interviewed Mr Jones' girlfriend, she mentioned they were going away for the weekend, maybe our killer didn't have a choice but to kill him early". The two detectives were quickly joined by a uniformed officer "what can you tell us about our victim?" Steven asked.

"Her name is Phoebe Hill formerly Phoebe Firth, she married in December last year to a Michael Hill, they live at Thirty-Eight Bond street" the uniformed officer responded.

"Who found the body?"

"a Mrs Hart, she was on her way to work in the early hours of the morning and spotted the body, she called it in right away. I spoke to her, but she didn't have any input, she was also a little shaken".

"Right, I think we better go and speak to Mr Hill" Steven said as he covered the body back up and left the crime scene. They entered the squad car and began to drive to the victim's home.

"I suppose we should let Mr Dawson out of holding" said Geoffrey.

"I don't think we should be too hasty Geoffrey; we can hold him legally for seventy-two hours."

"Do you think it could still be him?".

"I don't know what to think anymore."

The pair arrived at a small bungalow positioned in the middle of a cul-de-sac, flowers in the front garden and more hanging either side of the front door. The two detectives walked the path and knocked gently on the door, it was answered by an average height, large, ginger man with an untidy ginger beard sculpting his chin. "Are you Mr Hill", Steven asked

"yes" the man responded as a young boy ran up and hugged him from behind, peering round his waist to see the detectives.

"I'm detective Cooper and this is detective Osbourne, may we come in?",

"of course." replied Mr Hill as he opened the door fully and showed the detectives to a pair of armchairs positioned by a window in the living room. "What's all this about?" asked Michael as he encouraged his son to go and play in another room.

"I'm so sorry to tell you this, but your wife Phoebe was found dead in the early hours of this morning, I'm sorry for your loss" Steven said sympathetically. Mr Hill raised his hand to cover his mouth as he slumped in his chair, he stared blankly at the floor in front of Steven and remained silent. "Do you mind If we ask you a few questions?", Michael remained silent for a moment before returning eye contact with Steven and saying, "no, I don't mind"

"I know you and Phoebe married recently, but how long have you known her?"

"we met a few years ago, I was her lecturer at university, I know it's frowned upon for teachers to have relations with students, but I just felt this connection with her. I was going through some hard times when we met and she helped me through it, I wouldn't be the man I am today if I hadn't met her".

"Had she just finished her university course?"

"Yes, she graduated last year and was staring to look for a teaching job, she studied English and achieved a first-class degree".

"And the boy we saw earlier is he your son?",

"that's Sebastian, he's my son from a former relationship, he and Phoebe loved each other, this is going to crush him".

"Could you think of anyone who would want hurt Phoebe? Maybe a former lover?"

"no god no, Sebastian's mother sadly passed away five years ago, I turned to drink to cope with the situation, that's when Phoebe entered my life and helped me slowly turn it round".

"Anyone at the university that knew about your relationship?"

"no, we were very secretive, there was one time a chemistry student walked in on us kissing, but he pretended he didn't see anything, and we never spoke after".

"You mentioned you turned to drink, did you ever attended AA meetings to help with your addiction?".

"It never got that far, but it might have if I hadn't have met Phoebe."

"I think we've taken up enough of your time". Steven stood up from his seat as did Geoffrey, he handed Mr Hill a card "if anything comes up please give me a call, also if you need emotional support there's a grief counsellor's contact info on the back, take care of yourself Mr Hill".

"Thank you, detective." Steven and Geoffrey left the Hill's family home, as they did, Steven saw Michael's son playing in the kitchen, he could not help but think about Lily. Once back in the vehicle,

"when we get back, we can give Captain Luther a run down on this fourth case, hopefully if we throw a few ideas around we can find something" Steven said optimistically.

"Remember what you said about the cases being found in a particular order?"

"yeah".

"Well, what if the order is the stages they're at in their lives?" queried Geoffrey.

"What do you mean"

"Miss Willow had a drink problem and had started to recognise it, Mr Johnson was on his way to overcoming his addiction, Mr Jones had met a girl and started changing his habit for her and Mr Hill had overcome his drink issue with the help of his new wife. Obviously, Mr Hill is not our victim but someone losing their wife, especially in Mr Hill's case, is devastating for anyone, I can't help but think that it all fits too well. The suspect is targeting you after all, maybe this is their sick way of highlighting your past problems". Steven did not want this to be the case, but he could not help but think that it fit to well to be otherwise. The detectives arrived at the station around five P.M, Steven and Geoffrey headed straight to the briefing room and added the fourth victim, Mrs Hill, to the whiteboard of cases. A few hours past and eventually Captain Luther joined them "working late, what did you find?" he asked as he entered the briefing room.

"We interviewed the fourth victims' husband, they weren't much help, he couldn't think of anyone who would want to hurt his wife".

"I've come to the conclusion the people being murdered isn't as important as how much they relate to you detective Cooper".

"I had the same theory, great minds eh Ray" Geoffrey chirped.

"I understand that Captain, but that doesn't help us find the suspect, all it does is tell us that they know about my past".

"What it does tell us is that this person knows a lot about you, you've been five years sober, right?".

"Yeah"

"that means this person has known you for a longer time than Geoffrey has, maybe we need to work the suspect description angle, tell me everything you two can remember about the suspects appearance" said Captain Luther eagerly.

"Well, only Steven has seen him, other than the fuzzy security footage outside M&T lighting" Geoffrey added.

"What?" asked Captain Luther

"Geoffrey's right, I'm the only one who's seen him".

"So, we've only got, eyewitness accounts from you Steven, no one else?" both Steven and Geoffrey looked at each other. "Not to be funny Steven but how can we trust what you have seen, this person is clearly aiming everything at you, they could easily be playing you. The person you think you have seen may not even be involved"

"I'm not crazy Captain!" argued Steven.

"You've left me no choice Steven; I'm transferring the case over to detective Smith"

"but Captain."

"Stop Steven" interrupted Captain Luther "you think it's easy for me to do this to one of my best detectives, I think its best if you took some leave, You're too close to this. Let the rest of the squad deal with this hopefully a more objective look will help."

"Captain we're so close, I can feel it"

"Steven, either you take some leave, or I will suspend you, it's your choice" responded a defiant Captain.

Steven stared at Captain Luther in disbelief, but he knew that arguing with his commanding officer would be futile. He grabbed his things and stormed out of the precinct; Geoffrey followed closely behind. They reached the squad car and began to drive back to Geoffrey's apartment "why didn't you defend me Geoffrey?" asked an angry Steven.

"What do you mean?"

"when the Captain accused me of seeing things, you didn't step in, why?"

"Well, I haven't seen anyone only you have, I don't know what you are trying to imply but I'm on your side!" Argued Geoffrey.

"Your right Geoffrey sorry, maybe this case has gotten the best of me, perhaps its best to take a break and let someone else work it."

They arrived back at Geoffrey's apartment as the sun was starting to set, "I'll put the kettle on" said Geoffrey as he took his coat off and threw it over the arm of the sofa. He returned with two cups of hot tea and placed them on the coffee table in front of the sofa Steven was now slumped on. "Shall I order some food?" Geoffrey asked, Steven checked his watch, it read seven thirty, he double took before leaping from his seat and yelled "Claire!"

Chapter Eighteen: Grand Gesture

Steven grabbed his suitcase and ran to the bathroom, he threw on the best shirt he had packed and sprayed himself with some of Geoffrey's aftershave, he found on the bathroom shelf. He ran past Geoffrey and the hot cups of tea placed on the coffee table, grabbed the keys from the sideboard as he exited the apartment, jumped in the squad car and sped off to meet his wife at the Lychee palace. The sun was starting to disappear, and light rain drops began to fall on his car. "hurry up" he yelled at other road users and he tried to overtake, he arrived at the Lychee palace, parked the car and ran through the now heavy rain into the entrance of the restaurant. He checked his watch again, Quarter past eight, he swivelled his head to see if he could spot Claire, he could not. He asked the owner who was greeting people on the desk "Cooper reservation for seven thirty."

"your wife has already been and gone" she responded with compassion. Steven ran his hands through his hair and sprinted out of the building, through the pouring rain and back into his car. He drove away heading for his family home, his headlights penetrating the darkness in front of him. He skidded and slipped his way to his house, once outside he ran to the door and banged as hard as he could "Claire it's me, open up Claire please". No answer, he banged again "Claire I'm sorry, please can we talk" suddenly he heard a window open, he stepped from the little shelter the house was providing to see Claire was leaning out the landing window. "Five years Steven! Five years we've been going to that restaurant to celebrate our love, and you messed it all up because of your job."

"Claire, I'm sorry" replied Steven as the rainwater poured down his face and soaked his clothes.

"Sorry does not cut it Steven, I sat in that restaurant for over thirty minutes wondering if my husband was ever going to show up, the same husband that had said he would be there regardless."

"But Claire"

"I've had enough of your excuses Steven" Claire slammed the window closed. Stevens head dropped, his chin touching his chest, he slowly raised it back up to see Lily peering through the curtain. He blew her kiss and walked back to the car, he sat in the driver's seat, the rain beating on the roof of the car. He turned back to look at his family home before whispering the words "I love you Claire." He started the engine of the car and slowly drove back to Geoffrey's apartment, he exited the vehicle, ran through the rain and up the slippery metal stairs. He tapped on Geoffrey's door, it swung open, Steven tried to mask his tears, but even the rain dripping down his face could not hide them. He stumbled forward as Geoffrey put his arms round him "It's going to be ok Steven; it has to be." Geoffrey walked steven to the sofa sat him down and threw a towel, he grabbed from the bathroom, over his shoulders. He sat next to him rubbing his back, "I'll make us some tea", Geoffrey rushed off into the kitchen. Steven sat with his eyes fixed on the switched off television, he saw his reflection staring back at him. He could not believe how everything he had worked so hard to achieve had fallen apart so quickly. Geoffrey returned with the hot drinks and placed them on the coffee table "you are going to drink this one, aren't you?" Geoffrey asked trying to lighten the mood.

"Don't you want to get some sleep Geoffrey; you've got work in the morning".

"I called Cap when you were out and said I would take tomorrow off to be with you, I didn't want you to be on your own"

"thanks Geoffrey".

They sat awake for most of the night talking about everything that had happened over the past week or so. Eventually they went to sleep around two A.M. Stevens alarm woke him up at six, he snoozed it, he could not remember the last time he had done that, he placed his head back the sofa cushion, which was being supported by the arm, and fell back asleep.

Steven woke around midday, his neck sore from the sofa, his eyes sore from crying. He sat up and stretched out his arms and legs, rubbed his face with his hands and walked to the kitchen. He noticed the pile of paperwork, they had worked on over the past few days, sitting on the coffee table. He had to restrain himself from rifling through it and working the case, he ignored it and carried on walking to the kitchen. He made himself a coffee and returned to the sofa, he pulled his phone from his coat which was throw over the arm of the chair, to see if Claire had called. She hadn't, but there was a text from Captain Luther it read, 'look after yourself Steven, use this time to focus your energy on your relationship, we will solve this case and you will be back to work before you know it, Cap'. Steven knew that Captain Luther was right, but it was so hard for him to just switch off, for most of his life work was everything he had, he did not know what to do without it.

Geoffrey joined Steven in the living room, wearing a pair of black boxers. "Morning" he yawned "what's the plan for today?" he asked while rubbing the sleep out of his eyes.

"I'm going to take Captain Luther's advice"

"what's that then?"

"you'll see, just get ready".

The pair showered themselves, ate a late breakfast and left the apartment. This time Steven decided to drive "where are we going?" asked Geoffrey.

"There's a florist on the high street that sells Claire's favourite flowers, lilies"

"huh is that why her daughter is called Lily?"

"You are a good detective after all" Steven smirked. The pair arrived at the florist "I'll be right back" Steven said as he left to vehicle and entered the flower shop. He was greeted by a strong mix of aromas as he made his way toward the counter, where an elderly lady was standing "how can I help you?" she asked.

"I would like a bouquet of yellow lilies please" asked Steven with a large grin.

"Certainly" replied the shop keep "are they for someone special?"

"Someone very special" Steven responded as she walked off to start prepping Stevens request. He waited a few moments, sniffing flowers and perusing business cards until the lady came back. She returned with a large, beautiful, vibrant bouquet of lilies; Steven could not help but smile when he saw them. Claire is going to love these he thought, he paid for the flowers, thanked the lady and headed back to the car. He placed them on the back seat and entered the driver's seat "they look lovely" said Geoffrey with a hint of sarcasm "where to next?".

"The record shop on the corner of third" replied Steven.

"Once you've got everything you need, what are you going to do?" asked Geoffrey.

"Well, Claire is going to the Genesis gardens opening event tonight with a friend"

"oh, I thought you were going with her?".

"I was, but Lily's school are doing an intro day this evening for parents to meet the teachers and what not. My plan was to head to the house after she had left, set up all the things I bought for her. That way, when she returns from the gardens, she will be surprised by it."

"You're such a romantic Steven, aren't you"?

Steven smirked, he slowed the vehicle as he approached the vinyl store, he exited, and Geoffrey followed "I want to check out some vinyl's whilst I'm here" he said cheerfully. The pair entered the store, which had two customers standing in between long rows of records, they separated. Steven headed for the classic rock section, whilst Geoffrey walked over to the R&B vinyls. Steven quickly spotted what he wanted, Van Morrison, Brown eyed Girl single, he picked it up and looked round to find Geoffrey, once he spotted him, he headed towards him. "Found anything you like?" Steven asked,

"yeah, loads, but I don't have a record player".

"Why are you looking at vinyl's then?"

"because it's fun, anyway what have you got?"

"Brown eyed Girl, Van Morrison, it's Claire's favourite song".

The pair moved to the counter and Steven paid for his item, they left the store and got back into the squad car. "I take it you have a record player then?" asked Geoffrey as Steven pulled away from the store front.

"It's kind of old but it still works, one more stop, I'm going to get something for Lily, I can imagine this hasn't been easy on her".

"Is she going with you to the school event tonight?"

"no, it's just for the parents, she's staying at a friend's house".

They arrived outside the same toy store that Geoffrey had purchased Lily's birthday present from a week ago. Steven ran in and returned quickly with a large box, he placed it on the back seat, next to the flowers and the record. He jumped back into the driver's seat "ooooh, what did you get?" asked Geoffrey eagerly, Steven gave him a bemused look

"it's a Miss Millicent toy house, it goes with the doll Claire and I got her for her birthday".

"She will love that" responded Geoffrey.

Steven drove away from the toy store and headed back to Geoffrey's apartment, once there he collected the gifts he had bought from the back seat of the car. He shuffled up the metal steps outside Geoffrey's apartment and entered as Geoffrey held the door open. Steven placed the flowers in the sink, which he filled with a shallow pool of water, placed the record and the toy house on the coffee table and took a seat on the sofa. "Hey Geoffrey, have you made any more progress with Olivia?"

"no, I haven't seen her in a while".

"I would try and give you some more advice, but I might not be in the best position too." The two detectives smiled at one another. Steven checked his watch, six P.M, the closer it got to his grand gesture of love, the more nervous he became.

Chapter Nineteen:

Game Over

Steven dressed himself smartly, after all, he wanted to impress his daughter's teachers, he grabbed the items he intended to give to his wife and daughter and left Geoffrey's apartment. He drove over to the family home he had spent the last three years living in with his beloved family. Hidden under the large stone by the front door was a spare key, he opened the door to his home, walked in and took a moment. He had only been away for a few days, but he missed everything he had, he closed the door behind him and walked towards the living room. He placed the items in view of the front door, so his wife would see them as soon as she walked in. He took a pen from the coffee table and wrote on the label that was stuck to the gift wrap surrounding the colourful lilies. He placed the pen back down, took a step back and admired the gesture he had displayed for his wife and daughter. He left his family home and began his journey to Lily's school.

Meanwhile, Claire had arrived at the 'Genesis gardens' grand opening event, she was accompanied by Christina, a fellow teacher. They walked with the rest of the group, through the main entrance to the large glass structure, the room was humid, strong green spotlights helped illuminate the building. The structure separated into two paths; the centre and edges of the room was filled with tropical flora "this large tree, in the centre of the room, with the blackish-purple berries drooping from it is called an Acai tree" called the expert leading the group of visitors. "Its Latin name is Euterpe Precatoria, it is the most common tree in the amazon rainforest, making up one percent of the total tree's in the area". Claire and Christina walked further into the botanical gardens taking in all the colourful flowers. "you'll notice the plants growing from the Acai tree's" added the tour guide "these plants are called Epiphytes, they grow on other plants, they have no grounded roots and take nutrients from the plants they are attached to. Take a moment to peruse the other plants in the room, you'll see little plaques in the soil, they will tell you the type of fauna you would likely see in the amazon". Claire took her time walking the room with her colleague, taking in the smells, the colours and the information in front of her.

Steven had arrived at his daughters' school he was greeted by the headteacher, she was a short well-dressed woman, with short greyish black hair. She gave Steven a huge grin and shook his hand "hi, I'm the head teacher here at Hightower Community School, Mrs Atwell"

"I'm Steven Cooper, nice to meet you"

"nice to meet you too, if you walk into the foyer there is a desk which has a list of students names, if you find you child's name that'll tell you where you need to go" she said as she gestured Steven into the home of learning. Once in the centre of the foyer he noticed the table in the corner, he walked over and smiled at the man sitting at the desk "hi I'm Steven

Cooper, my daughter is Lily Cooper" he said as the teacher on the opposite side of the table began running his finger down the list of students names. "Cooper there she is, you're in science room three C, it's just down the corridor to your left and then turn right at the end". Steven smiled and walked the route he was given, once at the end of the bright hallway he turned right as instructed and looked at the door numbers as he passed, three A, three B, three C that's the one, he applied pressure to the handle and entered the class room.

Claire and Christina were encouraged by the botanist tour guide to enter the next room of the gardens. This room framed a large pond in the centre, this pond was filled with huge lily pads sprouting large colourful lilies. "These aquatic plants are referred to as Hydrophytes or Macrophytes, this distinguishes them from algae. The fish below use them as cover, they provide oxygen and food for some wildlife, like the small frogs you can see resting upon some of the pads". Claire lowered to gain a better view of the flora and fauna of the pond; she loved the colourful water lilies that had formed all around the pond. The room was silent, but for the sound of running water coming from the water features and the sound or croaking coming from the amphibians in the pond. They remained in the water plants section for around thirty minutes before the tour guide moved them on. "Everyone" he called "follow me into the courtyard here we will see many types of blossoms some you may be familiar with, and some you may not" the group followed the expert.

Steven was greeted in the school science lab by a tall, slim middle-aged man with ginger hair wearing a pristine white lab coat. "Hi, I'm Dr Rogers" he said as he reached out his hand

"I'm Steven" detective Cooper replied as he grabbed the teacher's hand and gently shook it.

"Take a seat anywhere and I'll explain the process of this evening". Steven looked towards the chairs and desk's facing towards him most of them were full, he noticed an empty space in the centre of the room. He walked over to the spot, awkwardly smiling at other parents as he did. "Now that all of you are here" bellowed Dr Rogers across the science lab "as you already know I'm Dr Rogers, I'll be you children's mentor for the year, that means if they need guidance, counselling, help with work or any other problems they come to me". Steven sat slumped in his chair, arms folded and occasionally looking out the window.

Claire, Christina and the rest of the group followed the expert out of the building and into a courtyard, brightly lit by floodlights. The temperature was mild as it was a summers eve, the sound of the water crashing down from the large rock garden in the centre of the courtyard filled the air, the area was cordoned off by various colourful potted plants. "Everyone over here" called the guide as the group followed "here we have a beautiful selection of hyacinth's, their genus in native to the Eastern Mediterranean. Move in a little closer and take turns to breath in their delightful scent". The gathering obliged and in small groups they began to take turns smelling the amazing flowers. Suddenly a large explosion occurred in the previous room "it's ok everyone, don't panic" called the botanist as he walked back to the room they had just left. Claire, along with her work colleague were stood at the back of the group, all were unsure what was going on as fear began to set in amongst the crowd. Christina screamed abruptly and the gathering spun round to see a shocking scene.

"I graduated from the university of capital city, let us see twelve years ago, I have been teaching here for three years and I've loved every minute of it. My PhD is in biochemistry, I spent many nights staring at that thing up there". He gestured towards a large poster which contained the periodic table, the group of adults let out a slight grumble of laughter. Steven slowly turned his head from the window towards the poster. He gazed blankly at it until his eyes fixed on the element with the atomic number thirty-two, Germanium, he could not help but think back to the Miss Willow case. The murder weapon being a Germanium pipe, which the forensic scientist said was odd. His eyes shifted across and up towards Neon, atomic number ten, the second victim Mr Johnson's body was moved to M&T lighting, which had bright Neon lights obstructing the view of the security camera. He continued this trend, above Germanium was atomic number fourteen or Silicon, Geoffrey had mentioned how the rocks covering the body of Mr Jones were from the old mining site which contained high levels of Silicon. Steven was beginning to piece this all together, he traced that row across two spaces to find Sulphur, atomic number sixteen, how could he forget Geoffrey's overreaction to the smell of the fourth crime scene. The strong smell of Sulphur hit the back of the throat, he thought, however the scientist explained Sulphur was odourless, that did not help with the smell. He went back through the elements in order of the body's, paying close attention to the chemical symbols, Germanium (GE), Neon (NE), Silicon (SI), Sulphur (S), Steven placed those symbols together GE,NE,SI,S. Instantly he knew that Claire would be in danger. He leapt from his seat and sprinted from the classroom, down the corridor, into the foyer and towards his parked car. He jumped in and quickly started the engine, he sped out of the car park and on to the road outside the school. He slid in and out of traffic, beeping his horn and gesturing at other drivers to get out of the way. Once he solved the puzzle, he knew instantly who the killer was. He arrived outside the gardens, left his car and sprinted into the building. He held up his badge to the scared woman on the front desk "where are they" he yelled.

"That way" she pointed towards the main entrance to the attraction "hurry". Steven burst into the tropical section of the gardens, he was hot and flustered and the humidity did not help, he progressed into the water plants room. He noticed the damage the explosion had caused; he quickly ran round the pond and out into the court. He noticed the group of people including Claire's friend Christina, huddled together and in shock, he walked slowly around the water feature in the middle, as he did, it revealed the scene that had everyone petrified.

His wife was being held at gun point by a masked assailant, he calmly approached, slowly raised his hand and said, "remain calm, everything is going to be alright". Claire screamed and jostled but it was no use, the assailants grip was tight. "ah, nice of you to join us detective Cooper, I was getting worried" said the masked person muffled by the balaclava.

"This is between you and me, let her go"

"you know I can't do that; I've worked too hard to not see out the job" Claire struggled again, but still no use. "You know, when I saw your wife had brought a friend instead of you, I thought, all of this had been for nothing, imagine my delight when I saw you arrive".

"You don't have to do this Dimitri" Called Steven. The masked man quickly removed his disguise to reveal a young man, with a strong jaw, furrowed brown and short dark hair.

"Well done detective, you figured out it was me all along, what gave it away?"

"Where do I begin, the first note you left me implied I had met you before, the people you killed represented my lifestyle before and after Claire, this means the killer must have known me for a while. The alias you used at the AA meetings, Mr Mendeleev the composer of the periodic table. I remember your passion for chemistry, so when I realised the elements had been used as clues, I only had one thought. It also makes sense that I wouldn't recognise you, the last time I saw you, you were just a kid".

"Very good detective, I was beginning to think all my work was in vein."

"I do have a few questions; how did you know we would be here tonight?".

"Think back detective, who sold your wife the raffle tickets?" Steven looked up in realisation "I rigged the raffle so you would win once that was confirmed my plan had begun".

"What about the fourth victim, they hadn't attended AA meetings how did you select them?".

"I'm not a big believer in fate detective, but that's the only way I could describe it, when I was studying at university, I walked in on a lecturer and a student being intimate, shall I say. I Monitored their relationship from afar, once I saw the way it was trending it was only a matter of time before I went about my duties".

"And you did all this to get back at me for putting Ivan Radzianko, your father, behind bars".

"Don't say his name!" cried Dimitri "you took everything from me, he was my only family, he was my mentor, he encouraged me to peruse my dream of science".

"Look how that turned out" interrupted Steven. Dimitri tightened his grip on Claire and forced the gun against her head, causing her to groan in pain.

"I don't think you're in a position to be making jokes detective". Steven was suddenly joined by an armed unit, which had been informed by a member of the tour group. Steven looked over his shoulder to notice their presence, he saw Geoffrey standing with his arms folded with a look of concern plastered across his face.

"Ok, I'm sorry" replied Steven "but this isn't going to end well for you Dimitri, put the gun down and we can talk."

"You think I planned on walking away from this?" questioned Dimitri as the armed unit began to surround him. "You took the one person from me I loved, the one who was everything to me, I think it's only fair I return the favour." Dimitri slowly applied pressure to the trigger of the handgun, which was pressed against Claire's head. A deafening bang followed "NOOO" cried Steven, he ran towards his wife as she fell to the stone floor. Bullets began to fly towards Dimitri, hitting him in the chest and sending him backwards into plant bed. Steven fell to his knees and held Claire in his arms, he could see the life slowly ebbing out of her "No Claire, please no, I love you Claire I love you so much". Her eyes slowly moved to meet Steven as she whispered the words "here's looking at you kid", the life left her body as she became heavy on Stevens lap. Steven held her for a moment, his tears dripping on her face, he placed her down softly and slid backwards till he felt the water feature prop him up. He sat with his head in his hands, distraught, inconsolable, heartbroken. Steven felt someone sit next to him, he did not look up, he felt an arm go around his shoulder and heard the words "it's going to be ok" whispered in his ear. He looked out the corner of his eye to see a teary-eyed Geoffrey sitting beside him "it's going to ok" he said once again.

Chapter Twenty:
Afterlife

Two weeks later,

"Lily come on, the car's outside" called Steven, Lily appeared at the top of the stairs. Steven looked up at his daughter, she was wearing a black dress, her hair was neatly brushed and a hairband with a bright yellow lily held it from her face. She walked down the stairs, using the handrail to keep her steady. Steven reached out his hand and Lily took hold of it, the pair walked from their family home, down the path and got into the dark black car positioned behind the hearse. The pair travelled to the funeral in silence, Lily spent the journey looking out the window of the car whilst keeping a tight grip on her dads' hand. The precession pulled up to the cemetery, which was filled with family and friends of the Coopers. Lily and Steven exited the vehicle and began greeting individuals, people from Claire's work, childhood friends and aunts and uncles filled the auditorium style seating arrangement. Lily and Steven their seats at the front,

"Claire Cooper, a loving mother, a caring wife, a loyal friend" said the funeral host, aided by the small microphone placed on the pedestal that looked out over the attendees. "We can all agree she was taken too soon", Steven reached to his left to hold Lily's hand. He saw her looking to the ground, her eyes fixed on one solitary place.

"Her passion was history, which she displayed through her teaching roll at Hightower Community school. Although her daughter didn't share the same passion, that didn't stop Claire from encouraging her from pursuing it."

A slight grumble of laughter befell the crowd, Lily's eyes remained fixed on the same location.

"She met Steven just over five years ago, the pair fell in love instantly. They shared the same interest, old films, family time, working too hard." Another groan of laughter resonated amongst the group as Steven wiped a tear from his cheek. "I understand that Steven has prepared a few words for the occasion" said the funeral host as she gestured him up to the pedestal. Steven released his grip on his daughter's hand, not before kissing her on the forehead. He walked up to the front of the audience and positioned himself by the microphone, he placed a small piece of piece of paper on the pedestal that he took from the inside pocket of his black suit jacket.

"As all of you know I'm not particularly good with public speaking, so I will keep it short. Claire was the love of my life; she was the best mother Lily could ask for and the best wife I could ask for. Things were not always great between us, sometimes I worked too much, but she always forgave me." Steven eyes began to flood with tears, he removed a tissue from his trouser pocket and dabbed the tears. "She encouraged me and Lily to pursue every dream we had, no matter how ridiculous. Claire made me want to be a better man, a better father, a better husband." Steven turned to the coffin, which was positioned behind him, and said "I will always love you Claire".

He stepped from behind the pedestal and began walking back to his seat. Before he could reach it, Lily took to her feet and grabbed Steven around the waist, she buried her face so that no one could see her tears, although they all shared her sorrow.

"We will now lower the coffin to the tune of 'Brown eyed girl' by Van Morrison, Claire's favourite song" called the funeral host. All in attendance stood to show their respect. The coffin, which was surrounded by vibrant yellow lilies, began to lower into the ground.

Steven stood by the exit of the cemetery, with Lily by his side. Attendees of the funeral began to leave as they did; they said their condolences to Steven. "I'm so sorry this happened Steven" said Christina as she leant in to hug him, "if you or Lily ever need anything, you know how to reach me", she knelt down to hug Lily before moving on.

"Take as much time off work as you need" said Captain Luther as he patted Steven on the shoulder.

"Thank you, Captain, I'm not sure when I'll return, my sole priority is to keep this one safe", Steven replied as he placed his palm atop Lily's head. Captain Luther gave the pair a smile before walking off.

"We still on for tomorrow night?" asked Geoffrey asked he appeared next in the queue,

"Of course," replied Steven "Lily has been going on about it for days".

"Really" said Geoffrey as he squatted down to Lily's level, "and what film are we going to see?"

"Casablanca" replied a tearful Lily.

"I'm looking forward to it" responded Geoffrey as he took an upright position, "you know I'm here for you Steven, whatever you need."

Steven smiled at Geoffrey as he moved away. More and more people gave their thoughts of love and hope to Steven and Lily. Once everyone had gone Steven and Lily received a lift back to their home from the funeral director. They arrived backed home, emotionally and physically tired, the pair slumped on the sofa and switched on the television.

The next evening,

Steven heard a knock at the door, he left the kitchen and answered it to see Geoffrey standing at the threshold to their home.

"Ready to go" he said eagerly

"one second, Lily Uncle Geoff is here."

Lily came running from upstairs, towards the door to give Geoffrey a big hug, she pulled away and Geoffrey noticed a book in her hand.

"What's that?" he asked, Lily became shy and left the conversation without saying another word, Geoffrey looked back at Steven.

"It's a history book, something to do with the Renaissance" replied Steven on Lily's behalf.

"Just like her mother" responded Geoffrey as he smirked at Steven. The threesome entered Geoffrey's car and began their journey to the drive through movie theatre showing classic films.

"Oh, I forgot to mention, I took your advice" said Geoffrey

"what's that?"

"I told Olivia how I feel, who knows I might end up getting hurt, but I've got to stop being afraid of my emotions."

"I'm proud of you Geoffrey, I hope it works out for the best"

"thanks, when do you think you'll return to work?"

"I honestly don't know if I will return, I need to put Lily first and I can't do that with my job"

"I understand" responded a sympathetic Geoffrey. The group pulled up to the movie theatre, parked the car and settled in to enjoy Claire's favourite movie.

I would like to dedicate this book to my family, without who, I am nothing.

Thank you for reading.

Printed in Poland
by Amazon Fulfillment
Poland Sp. z o.o., Wrocław

58424862R00136